Praise for Stephen Mangan and Anita Mangan's books

"A sure-fire way for kids to entertain themselves. What's more, it's also excellent for reading aloud"
LoveReading4Kids on *The Fart that Changed the World*

"A high-energy, brilliantly imaginative and laugh-out-loud tale that is guaranteed to blow away young readers"
Lancashire Evening Post on *The Fart that Changed the World*

"Just read the title ... that will draw them in. It's a bit naughty, a bit silly, a bit funny but you start reading and it's an adventure"
Holly Willoughby on *The Fart that Changed the World*

"Laugh-out-loud stuff"
Ray D'Arcy on *The Fart that Changed the World*

"An entertaining, heartfelt, problem-solving adventure"
Observer on *Escape the Rooms*

"A brilliant, clever, kind of genius book"
Graham Norton, Virgin Radio on *Escape the Rooms*

"[*Escape the Rooms*] is richly imagined and deeply heartfelt, and Anita Mangan's cartoonish and poignant illustrations capture the tone perfectly... It reminded me a little of *The Wizard of Oz*, with the children on a quest through different lands to get home" *Guardian*

"It's been described as a cross between *Alice in Wonderland* and The Crystal Maze and it manages to feel both classic and modern at the same time"
Good Housekeep

"A beautiful and exciting ad
Edith Bowma

Published in the UK by Scholastic, 2023
1 London Bridge, London, SE1 9BG
Scholastic Ireland, 89E Lagan Road, Dublin Industrial Estate, Glasnevin,
Dublin, D11 HP5F

ISBN 978 0702 31501 5

Printed by CPI Group (UK) Ltd, Croydon, CR0 4YY
Paper made from wood grown in sustainable forests and other controlled
sources.

1 3 5 7 9 10 8 6 4 2

www.scholastic.co.uk

THE UNLIKELY RISE OF HARRY SPONGE

STEPHEN MANGAN

ILLUSTRATED BY ANITA MANGAN

SCHOLASTIC

For Lisa x

CHAPTER 1

To say King Chisel was accident-prone would be an understatement. Hardly a day went by without him dropping something, tripping up or bruising himself. This morning, for example, was typical. The king woke up and rolled out of bed. Actually rolled right off the bed and on to the floor with a thump.

He'd done this so many times that his long-suffering aide, Honey Plunge, had placed several rugs on top of each other next to the bed to break the king's fall. The problem was that King Chisel kept tripping on the pile of rugs on his way to bed in the evening, careering head-first into the bedside cabinet, sending lamps, books, glasses, vases and alarm clocks flying. So Honey had been ordered to remove the pile of rugs and now every time the king

rolled out of bed he fell straight on to the hard wooden floor.

"STUPID FLOOR!" King Chisel barked, rubbing his shoulder, even though it really wasn't the floor's fault.

After getting up and straightening himself out, the king walked into the bathroom door. He had meant to open the door first but, still a little disorientated from falling out of bed, he'd missed the handle altogether. The door remained closed; he walked right into it.

"STUPID DOOR!" shouted the king, rubbing his nose, even though it really wasn't the door's fault.

Once safely inside the bathroom, he opened the cabinet above his sink, took out his toothbrush, brushed his teeth, bent down to drink some water from the tap, stood up and bonked his head against the still-open cabinet door.

"STUPID CABINET!" he yelled, rubbing the back of his head, even though it really wasn't the cabinet's fault.

King Chisel had always been clumsy, and his household staff had long ago learned to watch out for it. All sharp corners had discreet rubber pads attached to them, all windows were made with shatterproof glass, all knives were blunt, and so on. It was impossible to stop him hurting himself, but they tried to keep the damage to a minimum.

The king was also a danger to other people. He once accidentally poked the Bishop of Tug in the ear with a chicken and vegetable skewer. Years later, chicken dinners still caused the bishop to shake uncontrollably.

And, of course, there was the awful incident with Queen Myrtle.

After a thoroughly enjoyable royal wedding ceremony, Chisel and Myrtle were holding their reception on board the royal yacht, *The Unsinkable II*. The first royal yacht, *The Unsinkable*, had sunk a year earlier when Chisel steered it into a lighthouse.

King Chisel's clumsiness was already infamous, so his advisors had thought long and hard about the newly married couple's first dance. They didn't want the king standing on the queen's foot or poking her in the eye or knocking her to the ground. The dance routine had been worked out carefully weeks in advance, and the finest dance instructors in the land rehearsed daily with the young king and his bride-to-be.

On the night of the wedding, the king, thrilled to be marrying the woman of his dreams, became a little overwhelmed with joy and love (emotions with which he was unfamiliar). At the end of the dance, he spun his new queen so hard that she slid across the highly polished wooden deck, hit the handrail at the edge of the ship, flipped over and dropped into the ocean, never to be seen again.

It is fair to say that the king never recovered from this blow and never again permitted himself to feel either joy or love, but instead lived alone in the palace with only his loyal staff and a cat called Duke for company. From that moment he refused to appear in public and became mean, hostile and cantankerous.

The king, an only child, had never

remarried. He was now ninety-three, and his advisors were deeply concerned that he had no heir to inherit his Crown. They had found a living distant cousin of the king's, but Chisel was adamant he wanted to bring in fresh blood. For years they had nagged him about choosing someone to be the next monarch, and for years he had refused to discuss it.

But today, with a sore shoulder from falling out of bed, a sore nose from walking into the bathroom door and a sore head from cracking it on the cabinet, the king suddenly felt old and tired. He realized that they were right.

He needed an heir and he needed one soon.

CHAPTER 2

"What people don't understand about weightlifting," Gloria Squat-Further said to her classmates, "is how important chalking up is in the process. Chalk comes as liquid chalk, loose chalk, balls of chalk or blocks of chalk. You rub chalk on your hands to ensure a good grip on the smooth bar."

She clapped her hands together, creating clouds of chalk dust. The muscles in her arms rippled.

"And now I'm going to powerlift this barbell. It is equivalent to the weight of Laura, Patsy and Siobhan combined."

Laura, Patsy and Siobhan giggled.

"This is a little more weight than I lifted last month to win the Buxxo County Under-Thirteens Championship and would be a new personal best."

There was a polite round of applause.

"Thank you. I'm going to do a clean and jerk, which means I'll lift the barbell to shoulder height and then thrust it overhead so that my arms are straight. Oh, and please don't pay any attention to anything I might say during the lift. I go to some unusual places in my mind to summon the strength I need. Right. Here goes."

Gloria gave a little bow, walked around the barbell and stood before it. She dropped her head and closed her eyes. She started to breathe more heavily. Her fingers twitched and flicked. She lifted her powerful shoulders to her ears, then dropped them again. Opening her eyes and lifting her head, she slapped herself hard on the right shoulder with her left hand, then hard on her left shoulder with her right hand, leaving chalky handprints. She clenched her fists and started to vibrate violently, her whole body convulsing and jerking. She opened her mouth and screamed, a primal, rasping, tonsil-tearing scream that seemed to come from the very core of her being and scared the living daylights out of her audience.

Gloria lunged at the barbell, gripping and regripping it several times until she was satisfied. She carefully planted her feet underneath it and crouched down over the bar, knees bent, arms and back straight. There was a long pause and then, with a sudden explosive movement, her legs straightened, and the weight was up at shoulder level, her arms bent below it, elbows at her sides.

"GOULASH DOORBELL RUNNY TUMMY MUMMY!" she shouted. "ONION BUNION!

BOOSTER SEAT ROOSTER FEET!"

She dipped slightly, then rose again, her arms shooting skywards, propelling the barbell up and over her head, splitting her legs into a lunge to position herself underneath the enormous weight.

"SCATTER BATTER FLATTER MOONHEAD!" she bellowed.

Her whole body shook and trembled with the effort as she shuffled her feet together. Then she was standing upright triumphantly, arms in the air, holding the barbell.

"CHUTNEY ME, YOU FRUIT STALL INJUSTICE!"

Finally, she threw the barbell to the ground, where it went right through the school hall stage with a mighty splintering sound, leaving a gaping hole.

"Well, thank you, Gloria," said Mrs Trot, her teacher. "That was a marvellous 'show and tell'. We will ask Mr Blank to have a look at fixing the stage."

The door to the back of the hall burst open and in ran the maths teacher, Enormous Derek. Everyone turned to look at him.

"The king has launched a competition to find his successor!" he yelped. "The five best kids in the kingdom will fight it out to become heir of the realm!"

"I WILL WIN THAT FIGHT!!!!" bellowed Gloria so loudly that several of the class covered their ears with their hands. Gloria composed herself, bowed, curtsied, bowed again and left the stage.

CHAPTER 3

"My name is Huxley Beeline," said Huxley Beeline, "and I believe that my name, Huxley Beeline, should be written on your list."

The dentist's receptionist scanned the piece of paper in front of her and nodded. "Yes, Huxley. Please take a seat and the dentist will be with you shortly."

"Are you suggesting that I should remove a seat from your establishment?"

"I'm sorry, what?" said the receptionist.

"You asked me to 'take a seat'. Take it where?"

Huxley and the receptionist stared at each other for a moment. Huxley blinked several times behind his big round glasses.

"No," said the receptionist, after a moment. "I'd like you to sit down."

"Ah! Then I shall do that."

"Right," said the receptionist, picking up her pen. "Thank you."

But Huxley didn't sit down. He stood there looking at the receptionist. "I'd just like to ask – why will the dentist be with me?" he asked.

The receptionist put down her pen. "I'm sorry, what?"

"You said 'the dentist will be with you shortly'. But as I am going into his room and not vice versa, shouldn't you have said 'You will be with the dentist shortly'?"

The receptionist nodded slowly. **"I suppose that's right. Yes. You will be with the dentist. And ... please sit down."**

"Thank you. I shall."

Huxley sat down next to a man reading a newspaper. The headline on the front page, Huxley noted, read KING SEEKS FRESH HEIR. Huxley resolved to look into the matter. He pushed his glasses up his nose and straightened his bow tie. The man lowered his paper.

"Hot in here, isn't it?" he said to Huxley. "I'm sweating like a pig!"

"So you mean you are not sweating much at all?" asked Huxley Beeline. "While it is true that pigs do have a few sweat glands, they tend not to use them much in the cooling process. They don't sweat much at all. Their preferred method of lowering their temperature is to take a bath in mud. If you are sweating profusely, and I can see that you are – gross – the phrase you should use is 'I'm sweating like a pig iron'. This is the original phrase, which references the droplets of water that form on cooling globules of molten iron, globules often said to resemble pigs in their shape. Over time the phrase 'sweating like a pig iron' has, rather confusingly in my eyes, been shortened to 'sweating like a pig'. And furthermore–"

"Huxley Beeline, the dentist will see you now," interrupted the receptionist, to the man's great relief.

"Technically," said Huxley to the receptionist, standing and walking into the dentist's room, "the dentist is not seeing me now because I am yet to enter his room. He can't yet see me. The dentist will actually see me ... now. Hello, Mr Nee."

Huxley closed the door behind him, and all was quiet in the waiting room once more. The sweaty man sighed, picked up his newspaper and continued to read about King Chisel's competition to find an heir, which the king was calling the Crown Duels.

CHAPTER 4

"It's a competition," Jonny Mould heard one of his audience members whisper. "Each county in the land can put forward one child and then those five children go to the palace—"

"Shush!" hissed someone else. Their teacher, assumed Jonny. "Pay attention to the art."

"But, Miss, it's completely dark in here – we can't see anything!" came a girl's voice.

"That's the point! Throw the celery!"

"How can it be art if you can't see it?"

"Just throw the celery so we can go. All of you."

Jonny braced himself. Sticks of celery hit him on various parts of his body. One caught him full in the face.

"I don't get it..." said the girl.

Jonny sighed. He was doomed, it seemed, to be misunderstood. But then wasn't that often the fate of great artists? This show, "It's All a Bit Much", was, he felt, his greatest artistic achievement to date – but perhaps it was *too* good, too clever for his audience. His mum certainly hadn't understood it.

"So you're dressed head-to-toe in black, swinging upside down on the end of a black rope in a completely dark room, while people come in and throw celery at you?" she had scoffed.

"Yes," Jonny had said.

"And the celery is painted black?"

"Yes."

"And when it hits you, you sway back and forth?"

"Yes. It's a comment on the trials and tribulations of life, how we are buffeted by fate—"

"But you're not being buffeted by fate, you're being buffeted by celery."

"The celery represents fate. And the blackness represents death."

"And what does the rope 'represent'?"

"How we are all hanging by a thread. How precious life is. How dangerous. It's a metaphor."

There had then been a pause – such a long pause that Jonny had wondered if his mum had finally got it. He'd felt a surge of hope.

"**Well, I don't know,**" she'd said eventually, "**but I hope you're wearing clean underwear when you're doing it in case the rope snaps and you hit your head on the ground and the ambulance comes and they have to cut you out of your trousers and they see you are wearing dirty underwear and then what will they think of me? They'll think I'm the sort of mother who makes my children hang upside down from ropes in dark rooms in mucky underwear.**"

Now, Jonny, swaying gently, could hear the

school party start to file out and the schoolgirl resume her whispered conversation.

"I'm going to enter King Chisel's competition. Just imagine! Imagine if I win and I become queen!"

Or imagine if I won, thought Jonny. *Then they'd have to take my art seriously.*

CHAPTER 5

Gossie's aunt was standing on an ironing board. She had two knitting needles sticking into her shoulder, dark smudges all over her face, a live rabbit in a sack hanging around her neck and a crystal up each nostril.

"Anything?" asked Gossie.

Gossie's aunt shook her head.

"Ommmmmmmmmmmmmmmmmm turnips," chanted Gossie in an impressively deep and growly voice. She leapt from one foot to the other and then did some spinning on the spot. "Ommmmmmmmmmmm." She picked up a floaty scarf and twirled it above her head. "Ommmmmmmmmmmmmmm turnips turnips turnips. Ommmmmmmmmmmmmmmmmm ooh I feel a bit dizzy." She stopped spinning and looked up at her aunt. "Feeling it?"

Her aunt shook her head.

"Well, that is disappointing," said Gossie. "Maybe it's because Mercury is in retrograde."

"What does that mean?" asked Gossie's aunt and immediately wished she hadn't.

"I'm glad you asked me that," said Gossie, lighting another candle. There were now seventy-two lit candles in the room. "Mercury is the planet that rules our ability to communicate and express ourselves. For a period of about three weeks each year it appears to be moving

25

away from Earth – it doesn't really move, that's an optical illusion – and during that time it can severely influence us in a negative way. People get brain fog. Have you got brain fog?"

"Um ... I suppose."

"Exactly.   And anxiety. Got anxiety?"

Gossie's aunt looked at the needles sticking out of her shoulder. As she did so the ironing board she was standing on wobbled. "I have anxiety right now, yes."

"Headaches?"

"Well, not..."

"Disrupted travel?"

"No..."

"Falling out with friends?"

"Not that, no."

"Right, so you have all of those symptoms..."

"No, I don't."

"All of those symptoms," repeated Gossie, ignoring her aunt. "It's a classic case of Mercury being in retrograde. That's why the acupuncture didn't work."

She pulled the needles from her aunt's shoulder.

"That's why the lucky rabbit's foot didn't work."

She lifted the bag containing a rabbit from her aunt's neck.

"That's why the mystic sooty face massage

didn't work."

She licked her fingers and rubbed the soot off her aunt's face.

"That's why the healing crystals didn't work."

She plucked the crystals from her aunt's nostrils with a pair of tweezers, catching a couple of nose hairs as she did, causing her aunt to yelp.

"And that's why the sacred altar didn't work."

"You mean the ironing board?"

"Sacred altar," insisted Gossie, helping her aunt down. "I've got to say, Auntie, you have a very closed mind. This is all your fault."

"All my fault?"

"Yes," said Gossie. "You have to be open to the mysteries of the universe, Auntie. You have to allow the healing to work within you and through you. I sense strongly that you resisted everything here today."

"I just don't like standing on wobbly ironing boards at my age."

"**Mystic altar,**" insisted Gossie again. "**Anyway, I've got to go. I'll send you the bill.**"

"The bill?"

"Yes, the bill. Stop being such a downer! Honestly! Open your heart, Auntie. And then open your purse. You see, I'm going to the town hall now to enter the competition to be King Chisel's heir. I need some new clothes."

"You're – you're entering the competition?"

"That's right. I feel a deep connection to the throne and the palace. The universe is speaking to me, the throne is speaking to me, the entire country is speaking to me, and they are all saying, 'Gossie, you should be our new ruler.' Ommmmmmm."

CHAPTER 6

Harry Sponge was hiding in a cupboard with his little brother, Cy. His mum, Hilary, was under the bed; his dad was in the large green dustbin at the back of the building; Grandmother Sponge was trying – and failing, as it was far too small – to hide in the trunk in the hall; his sister, Maddie, was zipped up in a suitcase; and the dog, Lemon, was in a kitchen drawer.

The hammering on the front door resumed. Harry wondered if the door was strong enough to take it. There were, he guessed from the shouting, about five or six people out there.

"OPEN UP! We know you're in there! You're making it worse for yourselves!" came a gruff voice.

Harry could feel Cy trembling and clasped him more tightly, partly to reassure Cy and partly for his own comfort. This was the third time these men had come to the house, but he knew this was the visit when things would come to a head. The waiting had been exhausting. Harry hadn't slept in three or four days.

The banging stopped, and once more Harry could hear them trying to open the letter box he had nailed shut earlier that week.

"Last chance!" came the call. **"I'm going to count down from five and then we're coming in and no one is stopping us. FIVE."**

Harry knew the game was up but couldn't move.

"FOUR."

He also knew that the rest of his family were waiting for him to make a decision. Even though he was only twelve, Harry was in charge; they all instinctively understood that.

"THREE."

Harry's mind was confused and bewildered from lack of sleep. For once, he didn't know what to do.

"TWO."

From behind the kitchen door he could hear Lemon whimpering. He knew his mum and dad would be terrified. He could hear his grandmother still frantically trying to find a way to squeeze into the trunk.

"ONE."

Harry closed his eyes and pulled Cy even closer to him.

There were three thunderous bangs, the sound of wood splintering and the front door burst off its hinges, taking most of the door frame with it. Maddie screamed.

Six big brutish men swept into the house, ignoring the old woman half in and half out of the trunk in the hallway.

"Take it all," said the first man. "Take every single last thing."

Harry knew the men wouldn't hurt anyone in the house; they just wanted their belongings. And, of course, legally they had every right to take them. But still he stayed in the cupboard, unable to face the men and their contempt – or, worse, their pity. *Is this it?* he thought. *Is this, finally, rock bottom?*

No, he thought. He would turn things around.

In that moment, Harry knew that he needed to do something to reverse the fortunes of the Sponges. And that was when he saw a newspaper advert out of the corner of his eye: Want to Change Your Family's Future? Enter the Crown Duels!

CHAPTER 7

Even though he was ninety-three, King Chisel never missed his daily exercise session. In fact, he was convinced that the reason he had lived so long had been his consistent commitment to his daily workout.

Each morning, once he had risen and brushed his teeth, he put on the royal tracksuit. King Chisel had worn the same tracksuit for the last twenty-three years, and even though his housekeeper took great care when putting it through the laundry and had repaired it dozens of times, it was starting to fall apart. The housekeeper figured all the thread she had sewn into the tracksuit making repairs over the years now weighed more than the remaining original material.

King Chisel hated throwing anything away. He regarded it as one of life's greatest sins to put anything that was still useable in the bin and wore all his clothes until they could be mended no more. Everything in his wardrobe had been repaired many, many times. Jackets and trousers were covered in patches. Coats, jumpers and shirts had been sewn and re-sewn. All his socks were repeatedly darned until eventually they fell apart.

He was so committed to reusing things, he hated to see people buying anything new. **"Why buy a new shirt when you could wear an old one?"** was the way he looked at it. If any of his subjects or the palace staff showed up wearing new clothes, King Chisel would get extremely grumpy. **"IS THAT NEW?"** he would bellow in disgust. **"WHY ARE YOU BUYING NEW THINGS WHEN YOU ALREADY HAVE OLD THINGS?"** And he'd send them off to the shop to return the item.

What this meant was that if anyone *did* buy a new piece of clothing, they would try their hardest to make it look like an old piece of clothing before the king saw it. They would rub the edges of the cuffs and collars until they frayed; they would sew patches on to the elbows of jackets and the knees of trousers; they would deliberately rip pristine fabric and then sew it back up again.

Anyone who worked for the king knew the deal, but it was a lesson that others learned the hard way. King Chisel had once ripped the jacket and shirt off the Ambassador for Gunnerland at a drinks reception when the ambassador admitted he had bought them only the day before, especially for the occasion. King Chisel, who had been in a particularly bad mood that evening, had ordered the clothes be dispatched back to the shop immediately, and the poor ambassador had spent the rest of the evening topless and shivering.

This attitude brought King Chisel great

praise from anyone who worried about the planet and its dwindling resources, but it made him unpopular with those who designed and made clothes and with the shops that sold them.

The National Sewing Club was a big fan of the policy, and its crest featured a smiling tapestry depiction of the king, even though no one had seen him smile in decades.

With the royal tracksuit on, the king made his way down to the royal gym. There he was met by Randolph LaTouche, the royal personal trainer. Randolph knew better than to speak to the king this early in the day, so kept quiet as he handed him two squirrels.

The king grunted his thanks, sat on the workout bench and lifted one squirrel up into the air and then lowered it. He did this with the other squirrel in his other hand and his workout was underway.

The king had once owned a proper set of weights, the kind of weights you might find in a normal gym, but once these had started to fall apart after about fifteen years of use, he had refused to buy a new set.

"Waste!" he had barked. **"It's just something heavy to lift up and down! We can do that with anything!"**

He'd picked up the royal pet, which at that time was Jeffrey the Labrador, and had him weighed. Forty kilograms.

"I'll use Jeffrey instead of the forty kilogram weight."

And he did. He lifted Jeffrey above his head for three sets of ten. Jeffrey didn't seem to mind.

40

From then on King Chisel started using animals instead of weights. Randolph had drawn up a list, which he stuck to the wall of the gym so that the king knew which animal to use.

However, in recent years, the king hadn't been strong enough to lift anything heavier than the cat, so Ruth (the octopus), Sonia (the coyote), Gavin (the leopard), Patrice (the bulldog), Jermaine (the beaver) and Jeffrey were no longer needed and often no longer came into the gym in the morning. Ironically this had meant they spent a lot more time sitting around and eating, and they had all themselves put on quite a bit of weight.

Once he'd finished with the squirrels, King Chisel lay down flat on the workbench and Randolph handed him Mr Sparkle, the

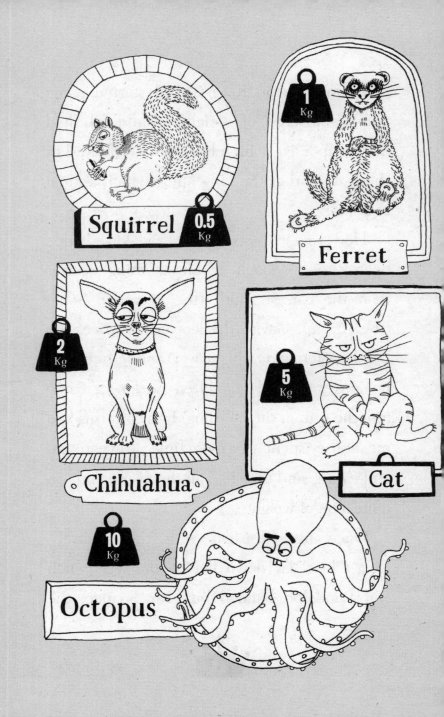

Squirrel 0.5 Kg

Ferret 1 Kg

Chihuahua 2 Kg

Cat 5 Kg

Octopus 10 Kg

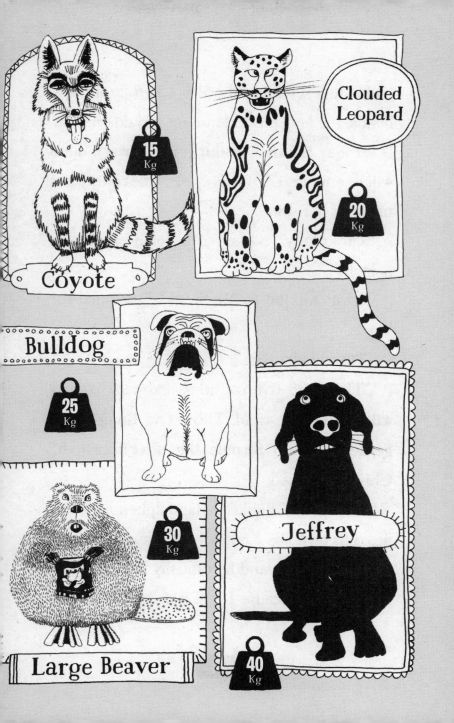

chihuahua. Holding the dog carefully in both hands, the king pushed him up and down.

"Today the first finalist for the crown duels will be announced!" he growled. "One county has made its decision."

"Oh really?" asked Randolph LaTouche politely.

"I was talking to Mr Sparkle!" boomed the king.

"I'm so sorry, sire."

"There are five counties, and each county will choose one child. Those five finalists will battle it out to become the next monarch," Chisel continued.

Mr Sparkle blinked. Randolph pursed his lips. His own lips – not Mr Sparkle's.

"One will win and become my heir. This had better work because I feel old and so tired. I

44

need someone to replace me."

Randolph wondered, and not for the first time, why the king had to shout everything. *No wonder you're tired, yelling all the time,* he thought but didn't dare say out loud.

"Five kids. I'm really going to test them!"

Randolph looked at the king's tracksuit with disdain. *How is it even still in one piece?* he thought but, again, didn't dare say out loud.

"I've got some pretty difficult challenges ready for them when the duels start next week. I'm going to enjoy making them suffer," said King Chisel.

He gently handed Mr Sparkle back to Randolph and sat up. Then he swivelled round to put his feet on the floor. This motion turned out to be the final straw for his ancient tracksuit bottoms. As the king stood, they fell apart and dropped to the floor, revealing his equally old royal underpants.

Randolph and Mr Sparkle looked in horror at the withered royal legs, the bony royal knees and the sagging royal Y-fronts.

CHAPTER 8

Honey Plunge looked out at the waiting crowd nervously. She was here to announce the child chosen to represent Grubshire County. King Chisel had entrusted her with overseeing the heats for the Crown Duels in each of the five counties. Nothing as exciting as this had happened to her before and she was determined to try and enjoy it.

Honey loved setting up the heats and making sure they were run properly and fairly.

However, she wasn't used to talking in front of large groups of people, so this was the one part of the job that slightly terrified her.

"I can trust you, Plunge," the king had said. **"I know how organized you are."**

He hadn't always called her Plunge. When she first started working for him, he'd referred to her as Honey. **"Pass me my book, Honey." "Oh, look at that sunset, Honey." "You know, Honey, I think I'll have a bath."** Until one day the king was pulled aside by the prime minister and asked if he was thinking of making the aide his new wife.

"What?!" the king had exclaimed.

"I certainly am not! Why do you say that?"

"Because you keep calling her 'Honey'!" the prime minister had sniggered.

"Yes. That's her name."

But the prime minister hadn't believed him and kept nudging the king and winking in a suggestive manner and tapping the side of his nose and saying things like **"Your secret's safe with me"** and **"Can I be a pageboy?"** in an incredibly irritating way. In the end, the king had decided he either needed to fire his prime minister or to stop calling Honey "Honey" and call her Plunge instead. He chose the latter, but often regretted he hadn't chosen the former.

From then on Honey Plunge was just "Plunge".

The king hadn't told Honey Plunge *why* he'd made this sudden switch, so for a while she worried whether she had done something wrong and if King Chisel was unhappy with her. She'd decided to work harder than ever and took great pride in working for the king.

And her hard work had not gone unnoticed. King Chisel trusted her more than anyone else at the palace.

Now, as Honey stood at the side of the stage, she suddenly remembered that she had recently eaten a white bread sandwich filled with chicken, spinach and sesame seeds. She knew that white bread, spinach and sesame seeds are some of the worst foods for getting stuck in your teeth. What with all the rushing around the counties overseeing the heats, she hadn't had time to check herself in the mirror and she fretted that her mouth looked like a crime scene.

"And now, let's welcome to the stage, Honey Plunge!"

It was too late now. Taking a deep breath, Honey strode out to the middle of the stage, feeling a little wobbly in the new shoes she'd bought for the occasion (and kept hidden from the king). When she reached the microphone, she smiled, taking care to keep her lips together in case she revealed her teeth.

There were about five hundred people there. Some photographers at the front started taking pictures. The shortlisted children stood to the side waiting.

"Hello, ladies and teeth!" Honey said. **"Ladies and gentlemen. Sorry. Not teeth – gentlemen. Hello, everyone. It is my great pleasure to announce the child that will represent Grubshire County at the Crown Duels."**

She was trying to speak without opening her mouth too much, so she was a little hard to understand.

"The children have been competing in a range of tests – logic, physical, general knowledge, stamina, balance, dance, singing, maths, science and so on. We wanted to find the candidate with the best overall levels of teeth. *Skill.* Best overall levels of skill. Normal skill. Not teeth skill. Whatever teeth skill is!"

She tried to laugh casually, then realized she was showing her teeth so stopped.

"Anyway, let's get on with it. From the ten children shortlisted, the one that you, the county of Grubshire, have chosen to go into the finals of the Crown Duels is..."

This was the moment Honey had obsessed

over ever since she had been told it was going to fall to her to announce the winning candidates. She'd decided it would make it extra exciting and extra special if she left a long pause before saying the winning name.

So she paused.

For quite a long time.

With her mouth clamped firmly shut to hide her teeth.

This really is making it extra exciting! she thought to herself.

"HURRY UP!" someone shouted.

"What? Sorry! Yes! Teeth!" Honey blurted. **"The winner is Gloria Squat-Further."**

Gloria stepped forward from the line of children with her strong arms raised above her head. She looked towards the sky and unleashed her most blood-curdling roar.

Three of the other children started crying.

Honey Plunge ran off the stage, her face burning with embarrassment. That had not gone the way she had hoped. Before heading to Wurtleshire County and the next announcement, she checked her teeth in the mirror and had her worst fears confirmed: a huge piece of spinach was stuck between her two front teeth.

CHAPTER 9

Harry Sponge listened carefully. The front door had slammed shut several minutes ago, but he wanted to make sure the men had really gone. Apart from Lemon whimpering in the kitchen drawer, he couldn't hear anything.

"OK, let's go," he whispered to Cy.

He pushed open the cupboard door and the two of them emerged blinking into the light. Cy ran straight to the kitchen, opening the drawer to lift Lemon out. The dog licked

Cy's face enthusiastically.

Harry took in the aftermath of the men's visit. They had taken everything that wasn't attached to the wall or the floor – sofas, chairs, tables, pictures, rugs, beds … everything. It looked like a house that no one had lived in for some time.

In the hallway, his grandmother was wedged into the corner, standing with her face to the wall. The trunk she had been trying to get into was gone. When Harry put a gentle hand on her shoulder, she jumped. Seeing Harry, she broke into a small smile, but he could tell she was on the verge of tears.

Hearing movement, Harry's parents had left their hiding places and joined Harry and his grandmother in the hall.

"At least **it'll** be easier to keep the place tidy," Harry said, with a rueful smile.

"Yes," said his mum. "**I won't lose my keys ever again! Because I don't have any now!**"

"**I'd put the kettle on**," said Harry, "**but I suspect they took that too.**"

"**Yes, they did,**" said Maddie, coming into the hallway.

They all stood in silence for a moment.

"I'm sorry," said Harry's dad.

"You don't need to..." began Harry.

"I don't ... I don't need to, but I'm saying it again. I'm sorry. This is all my fault."

"Dad..."

"Let me speak. Things seemed to get worse and worse really slowly – and then suddenly they got really bad really quickly. For a while I thought I was in control and then I wasn't at all. I couldn't stop it happening and now we have no money, and I can't see how we're going to get any again..."

He looked at the floor, unable to speak any more. Harry's mum put her arm round his dad's shoulder. Everyone stood quietly for a moment.

"I'm going to make this better," said Harry

firmly. "The king is running a competition to choose the next king or queen. I'm going to enter it and I'm going to win and I'm going to get us out of this mess."

He grabbed his coat and ran to the door.

CHAPTER 10

"The child the county of Wurtleshire has chosen to represent it at the Crown Duels," said Honey Plunge, **"is Huxley Beeline!"**

Huxley Beeline had known he was going to win. He had done the calculations in his head already and his assessment was that there was no way he could have lost. The only round in the competition that he probably hadn't won was the obstacle course.

In fact, he *definitely* hadn't won the obstacle

course round because he hadn't even attempted it. He had calculated that there was a good chance he would come near the bottom in that round. Points for each event were only awarded for finishing in the top fifty – and, as four hundred and seventy-two children had entered from his county, he was never going to achieve a top fifty place in this event. Plus, he had estimated that there was a fairly high chance that he might get injured attempting some of the more difficult obstacles and figured it wasn't worth risking a broken arm when he wasn't going to score any points anyway. And it would have meant taking off his favourite waistcoat and that felt unnecessary.

Huxley had consulted the rule book in case he could be disqualified for not completing every event and found nothing. He had then memorized the entire rule book so that he could recite it if necessary. Huxley had a fantastic memory. He learned all twelve pages of the rule book in one hour and twenty-three minutes.

Huxley stood at the side of the stage. He estimated the distance between himself and Honey Plunge. Then, giving a rough value in metres per second to his walking speed, he applied the formula Time = Distance/Speed to arrive at what felt like a reasonably accurate approximation of how long it would take him to walk from where he was to Honey: 4.21 seconds.

Four seconds or so also seemed to him a reasonable guess for how long it would take Honey to complete the sentence in which she announced the winning child. *Unless,* thought Huxley Beeline, *Honey Plunge did that really annoying thing where people*

paused for ages just before saying the winning name in a misguided attempt to build tension and drama.

Huxley's dad had died when Huxley was only just nine years old, and he missed him more than he could express. It had happened exactly one month after Huxley's ninth birthday. Huxley had calculated that he'd had a dad for 3,319 days. Or 79,656 hours. Or 4,779,360 minutes. Or 289,761,600 seconds, which sounds like a lot, but now that his dad was gone and he'd never see him again it didn't feel like nearly enough.

Huxley was highly sensitive to the fact that everybody only had a limited amount of time in their life. Time, he knew, travelled in one direction only – forward. Any wasted moments, any boring moments, any tedious moments could never be reclaimed. They were gone for ever. Time, he felt deep in his bones, was precious and it should not be wasted. Waiting as someone paused for pointless dramatic effect when, for example, announcing the winner of a painting competition or a baking competition or *any* competition irritated him beyond belief.

And people taking ages to get to the stage after being declared winner annoyed him. *You've won, hurry up and get on with it!* he'd think. Watching them gasp in astonishment, watching them hugging their friends and/or family, watching them walk slowly up, high-fiving people and punching the air – all one massive waste of precious time.

Huxley was determined to waste neither his nor anyone else's time today, so as Honey began the sentence, **"The child the county of Wurtleshire has chosen ..."** Huxley began walking towards her.

As Honey said, **"... Huxley Beeline!"** Huxley Beeline was at her side. Honey had not seen Huxley coming, so his sudden appearance caused her to jump in surprise.

Without breaking stride, Huxley took the small trophy, said **"Thank you,"** left the stage, walked out of the door, and went home to tell his mum.

CHAPTER 11

King Chisel sat down to a very late breakfast of black pudding and cheese washed down with cold tea and salt. He'd been eating the same breakfast every day for nearly ninety years. Honey figured the king must have no taste buds because while black pudding and cheese was a strange choice, tea with salt in it was outright weird. Not that Honey would ever dare say such a thing to King Chisel.

As the king was putting more salt into his

tea, he spilled a little on the tablecloth. Being a superstitious man, he believed spilling salt was bad luck and that he needed to throw a little over his left shoulder. The king believed in a lot of superstitions like that. He thought it bad luck for a black cat to cross your path, so he had black cats banned in the kingdom. He thought bad things would befall anyone who walked under a ladder, so builders had to get special permission to use them. His mother had told him it was bad luck to put shoes on a table, so he passed a law banning his subjects from putting their shoes on a table of any kind at any time.

But it didn't stop there. He had plenty more superstitions – and plenty more laws. Laws banning his people from flipping cooked fish, from kissing in doorways, from whistling indoors, from toasting anyone's health with a glass of water. There were no houses with the door number thirteen, hairdressers were closed on Saturdays and men weren't allowed to eat goat meat because King Chisel worried it might cause them to grow beards. He hated beards.

So now, when he spilled some salt, he felt he had to act. He went to pick up a few grains of salt but absent-mindedly grabbed the whole solid silver salt cellar and threw that over his left shoulder instead. It sailed through the air and hit the prime minister, who was at that very moment entering the room, right between the eyes, causing him to collapse in a heap.

The prime minister was a devious man who had become prime minister mainly because of a fart machine. His name was Winston

Bernard Alfonso Charles Gordon Gideon Demerol Smitherington-Piffle, but he insisted everyone call him Bernie. He was a mean, nasty character, but by getting everyone to call him a fun and cuddly name like "Bernie", he had persuaded lots of people that he wasn't mean, nasty and unpleasant at all, but that he was fun and cuddly.

And then there was the fart machine.

Whenever the prime minister was asked questions by serious and clever journalists about serious and important topics, instead of answering these questions, he would press the button on his fart machine. The fart noises it produced were realistic. Lots of people found farting much more entertaining than sensible answers to serious questions. "Farting Bernie", as he was affectionately known, had become extremely popular and had won the election by loads of votes, despite having no real clue what he was doing.

Some people had wondered whether it might be better to have a prime minister who was sensible and clever and had answers for the difficult issues that the country faced, but mostly people said, **"Oh, be quiet and listen to the farts! They're hilarious!"**

When Farting Bernie was hit in the face by the salt cellar and collapsed, he fell on to the fart machine and it let out the sound of a loud, long, wet fart. King Chisel, who hadn't realized he'd thrown the salt cellar at all, heard this and thought perhaps it might have been *him* who had farted. He shrugged and had another slurp of salty tea. *Needs more salt,* he thought, and looked around for the salt cellar.

Farting Bernie, meanwhile, scrambled to his feet and picked up the silver salt cellar. He presented it to King Chisel.

"What are you doing with my salt cellar, Smitherington-Piffle?" boomed the king, grabbing it and pouring more salt into his tea. He saw straight through Winston Bernard Alfonso Charles Gordon Gideon Demerol Smitherington-Piffle's attempt to make himself seem loveable when he wasn't, and, he never called him Bernie. He would have happily sacked him, but the prime minister was chosen by the people and, even though the king wielded most of the power in the country, such a move would have been deeply unpopular.

Farting Bernie didn't know how to answer this question so pressed the button on his farting machine. A quiet, melancholic, droopy fart noise came out. King Chisel stared at him with contempt.

"What do you want, Smitherington-Piffle?"

"Oh. Ah. Crikey. Jeepers," stumbled Farting Bernie. "I, um, come with news, er, of the Crown Duels, Your Most Resplendent Majesty."

"Stop snivelling, you loathsome man-baby, and just tell me what the news is!" retorted the king, grumpy because he'd now put a little too much salt into his tea.

"It would give me a warm and delicious feeling in my tummy-tum to do so," said Bernie. "It makes me all hot-chocolatey and gooey inside to do you service of any kind, your gracious and most fragrant—"

"GET ON WITH IT!"

Bernie jumped. He toyed with the idea of

a fart noise but decided against it.

"Of the five counties in your glorious kingdom, sire, four have completed the process of choosing a contender to represent them at the Crown Duels."

"Who are they? Names!"

"First is Gloria Squat-Further, Your Massive Maj, a rather impressively structured child. Strong and smart too. Our research tells us she would run through a brick wall to win at, well, anything."

"Next?"

"Huxley Beeline, sire, a child possessed with supreme intelligence and an attention to detail that borders on the fanatical. He has contacted my office no fewer than forty-six times in the last few days to clarify various points and to correct inconsistencies in some of our statutes."

"Next?"

"Gossamer Fountain. Known as Gossie. She claims, among other things, to be able to see into the future. When I spoke to her to congratulate her on her success, she kept saying, 'I knew you were going to say that.' It was, I have to confess, quite irritating. When I made a little joke and asked if she already knew whether she was going to become our queen, she said I was a very closed person."

"Next?"

"Jonny Mould, you dazzling regal entity. A performance artist."

"A WHAT?!"

"A performance artist, sire. He explores themes of mortality and destiny in his work. Celery features too."

"Heaven help us. And the final candidate?"

"Ah," said Smitherington-Piffle, and looked at his shoes.

"Are your shoes going to tell me?" asked the king grumpily.

"Ha! No, sire."

"Then don't look at *them*, look at *me* and tell me who the fifth candidate is going to be."

Farting Bernie mumbled something.

"WHAT? SPEAK UP!" bellowed the king.

"Breege County," Bernie said, sheepishly. "They haven't decided yet."

The king started breathing heavily in and out of his nose. This was a bad sign, the prime minister knew. This meant the king, already an irritable man, was about to properly lose his temper. And when the king lost his temper, he really lost his temper.

Once he'd got so cross at the royal astronomer that he had shoved the royal telescope up the royal astronomer's nose.

Once he'd got so angry when trying and failing to learn a song on the piano that he'd pushed the piano out of a second-floor window. It had smashed into a million pieces when it hit solid ground.

Once he'd got into such a rage trying to draw his cat that he had thrown the piece of paper on to the floor and jumped up and down on it for three hours. The cat was so terrified it ran away and has not been seen again.

So, when the king started breathing heavily in and out through his nose, Bernie was immediately concerned.

"Sire, it's all in hand. They had a ... small mix-up but are holding the final heats any

minute now. Honey Plunge is there to make sure they go without a hitch. All shall be well."

The king let out a low growl. The prime minister cast frantically around for something to calm him down.

"And the best news, Your Royalty, is this..."

Bernie pressed the button on his machine and it delivered a long, low, quivering fart.

Bernie guffawed. The king scowled.

"It's funny because..." explained the prime minister, losing confidence as he spoke, "... it sounds like ... a fart."

BERNIE'S FART MACHINE

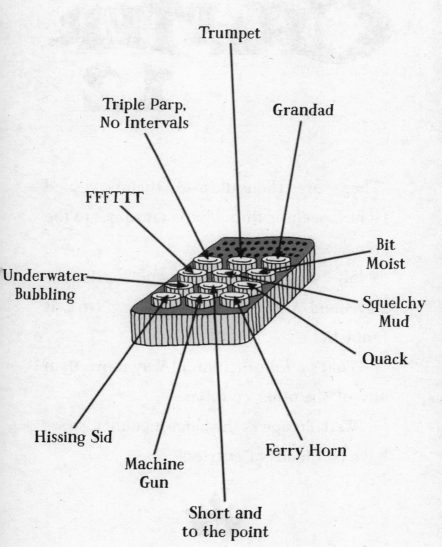

Trumpet

Triple Parp,
No Intervals

Grandad

FFFTTT

Bit
Moist

Underwater
Bubbling

Squelchy
Mud

Quack

Hissing Sid

Machine
Gun

Ferry Horn

Short and
to the point

CHAPTER 12

"There are thousands of them!" gasped Honey, peeking through the curtain into the arena.

"Six and a half thousand!" said the stagehand standing next to her. "Isn't it fantastic?"

"That's a *lot* of children! Way more than any of the other counties."

"Well, Breege is the biggest county, so we have had loads of entries!"

Honey could feel the panic crashing through her. Like someone had reached a hand into her chest and … no … more of a pain in her chest, racing heartbeat, shaking. A wave of fear that flooded her so quickly she was dizzy with it.

It wasn't just the size of the crowd. It was also a feeling that things had to go wrong at some point and that they were bound to go wrong at the worst possible moment.

"I'm going to … a breath. Some air," Honey mumbled.

"Don't go far," said the stagehand. **"We need to get started shortly."**

"I won't be long."

As calmly as she could, Honey pushed open a nearby door with her clammy palm and found herself outside. She slammed it shut behind her and sank down, head in hands, trying to breathe normally.

CHAPTER 13

Farting Bernie sat alone in the grand office that comes with the job of prime minister. Outside in the corridor he could hear several of his colleagues laughing and joking with each other and he hated them for it. Although he had perfected the skill of making others laugh and was good at *pretending* to enjoy himself, inside he was … dead.

For a moment, he wondered what it felt like to lose yourself in laughter, to giggle

uncontrollably. He could not imagine it.

Another peal of laughter made him tense further. They were probably laughing at him, he thought. Probably sharing a joke at his expense. He hated them. He hated everyone. What would make him feel better? He called in his assistant.

"**Tell the Theatre Royal that it has to close for ever,**" he told her.

"**Oh. They'll ask why.**"

"**Tell them there's not enough money.**"

"**But there *is* enough money.**"

"**I know and I don't care. Do it.**"

His assistant left. *That'll do*, he thought. *If I can't enjoy myself, at least I can stop others from doing so.* And for a few seconds Bernie felt a small glow of dark pleasure; for a few seconds the emptiness inside him receded.

Then he called in his assistant again.

"And I want new wallpaper."

"Oh, right. Didn't you redecorate the office a few months ago?"

"I don't think you heard me, you wretched little fool – I WANT NEW WALLPAPER. My face in gold. With 'Bernie' underneath. In gold. On a gold background. Over and over. That's the pattern."

"But if your face is gold and the name is gold and the background is gold, if everything is gold, won't it just be ... gold?"

"DO IT."

"Yes, sir."

CHAPTER 14

Harry came tearing round the corner. There it was, up ahead. The building where the Breege County heats would be held. He was going to make it. Just.

He could hear the sound of excited children talking, laughing and shouting from inside the arena.

The entrance *must* be around the next bend. It felt as though he had run around the whole perimeter of the enormous building towering over him. He passed a woman sitting in a doorway with her head in her hands. He thought about stopping to ask her for directions, but there really wasn't time.

As he ran past the woman, though, he sensed something wasn't quite right. Perhaps it was the way she was sitting or the way her shoulders were heaving up and down. He slowed and stopped. He turned back and walked over to her.

"Excuse me," he said gently.

The woman lifted her head from her hands and looked blankly up at him. Like he wasn't really there.

He said nothing, waiting for her.

"I'm sorry," she said, after a moment.

"That's OK," he replied with a small smile. He sensed this woman was struggling with something. He waited for her to speak.

"Do you want to sit down?" she said at last.

"OK."

Harry sat down next to her.

After a few seconds, she seemed to be breathing less heavily. She turned and smiled at him. "Thank you," she said.

"I didn't do much." He grinned.

"You did exactly the right amount. What's your name?"

"Harry Sponge."

"That's funny! I'm Honey Plunge. We rhyme."

"We do!"

Honey took a deep breath in and exhaled slowly. "Right, things to do."

"Yes! Me too!" Harry stood up. "Nice to meet you, Honey Plunge."

"And you, Harry Sponge."

She turned and walked back through the door and Harry realized he hadn't asked her about the entrance to the arena. Never mind. He'd better run!

He sped on, rounding the next corner, and there was the entrance. He raced over to it. A man was closing the door.

"Hi, sorry, excuse me!" panted Harry. "I'm entering the Crown Duels trials. Where do I go, please?"

"You're too late."

"What?! What time is it?"

The man looked at his watch. "Two p.m. and twenty-three seconds."

"So I'm twenty-three seconds late?! Can't you let me in?"

"This," the man said haughtily, "was the

first test. Getting here on time. How can you expect to beat thousands of others to be the next king if you can't even turn up at the right time? You blew it, sunshine. Now scram."

CHAPTER 15

The prime minister crept into the king's office for the afternoon briefing. He prayed that the king had cooled off since their last conversation. He was surprised to find the king's doctor, Barbara Face-Problem, there.

"Where's the king?" Bernie asked. "Is he all right?"

"He asked me to talk to you. He stubbed his toe on a chest of drawers in his bedroom."

"Oh no. He'll be grumpy."

"Then, as he was hopping over to the bed to sit down, he slipped on a rug and fell backwards, flinging the shoes he was holding into the air. They smashed into the chandelier, shattering it. Thousands of glass shards fell to the floor and as the king scrambled to stand up, he got cuts on his hands and knees."

"Oh, that's not good," said Bernie.

"That's not all. He was pulling himself up by clinging on to the curtains when the curtain pole snapped and he fell over backwards, hurting his bottom."

"Oh no."

"He rolled over on to his front and accidentally knelt on the cat's tail."

"We don't have a cat, do we?"

"The cat that's been missing for years.

Turns out it was hiding under the king's bed. Anyway, it's still a bit nervous and it jumped out and dug its claws into the king's bald head. That's when I ran in..."

"Right."

"I helped him to his feet but by then the cat had slid down his face over his eyes. The king screamed, 'WHO TURNED THE LIGHTS OUT?' and ran to the light switch. But because he couldn't see where he was going, he walked out of the door and fell down the stairs. Head over heels all the way to the bottom. It's a very long staircase."

"Yes, I know."

"Seventy-two steps."

"He must have been shaken up."

"That wasn't the end of it."

"Crikey!"

"The cat had hung on to his scalp all the way down. As the king lay there at the bottom of the stairs moaning, the royal dog..."

"Lord Woofington?"

"Yes, Lord Woofington, he heard the commotion and came to investigate. When Lord Woofington saw the cat, he charged at it. The cat got away, but the wooden floor in the hall is incredibly shiny and slippery and the dog couldn't stop. As you know, Lord Woofington is a Great Dane and they are *big* dogs, so when he slammed into the king, the two of them slid together across the hall, past the portrait of His Majesty and out of the front door (which was open because it was such a beautiful day), off the front steps and into a wheelbarrow full of manure that was there because Larry Bing-Bong the gardener was fertilizing the rose bushes by the steps."

"Golly."

"That wasn't all."

"It wasn't?"

"The king and Lord Woofington, both now covered in cow poo, jumped out of the wheelbarrow and ran towards the royal pond to wash it off. But the king didn't see the royal beehives that had been placed on the front lawn while they were cutting down the big tree in the back meadow that got damaged in the storm, and he ran straight into one. The whole beehive collapsed and split open and the bees inside went berserk, stinging His Royal Highness about a thousand times."

"I can't believe it!"

"So he staggered to his feet, ran to get away from the bees, stood on the end of a rake which Larry had left lying on the ground, and the rake handle boinged up and smacked him in the face."

"That's incredible! Is he all right?"

"Well, he's got a black eye, he's been stung a thousand times, he's got claw marks on his head, his toe hurts, he's covered in bruises and cuts and he slightly smells of poo. What do you think?"

"I think I'll ... come back another time."

"Good idea."

CHAPTER 16

Harry knocked on the bathroom door.

"Dad?"

No answer. Maddie had told him his father was in there. He tried again.

"I'm so sorry, Dad, but I got to the heat too late. My fault. I blew it."

Still nothing from inside.

"Dad? Can you forgive me?"

A quiet voice from the bathroom said, **"Of course I can, Harry. I don't blame you for**

anything. How could I? Thanks for even trying. Now, could you please leave me alone for a bit?"

"I don't want to leave you alone. And I'm not going to."

There was a moment of silence, then Harry thought he heard a small sigh. The door unlocked. His father, Jonathan, looked ashen.

"None of us blames you for what happened, Dad."

"That's good of you."

"It's not good of us. It's just the facts. You were unlucky. We all were. Now could you come into the sitting room and be with us?"

"I don't want to."

"We want you to."

Jonathan shrugged and started to close the door. Harry placed his foot across the threshold so that it wouldn't shut.

"No. Don't you get it, Dad? We don't blame you."

"Harry," said Jonathan sharply, his eyes filling with tears. "It's great that you don't blame me. But the fact is I blame myself. That's what I can't live with. I blame myself. I hate myself. And I can't get away from it, from me, from these thoughts. So thanks, Harry, but I'm staying in here for now. Move your foot, please."

He shut the door firmly and locked it. Harry pressed his forehead against the door frame.

If only he'd made it to the heat in time.

CHAPTER 17

King Chisel was being served food by Doctor Barbara Face-Problem. Or rather, the doctor was holding up a glass of protein smoothie for him to drink from a straw. Covered in stings, cat scratches and bruises, the king looked a sight.

He slurped at the drink noisily and messily. Barbara tried not to show her disgust.

"The last contestant is being chosen in Breege County today," she said. **"But are you**

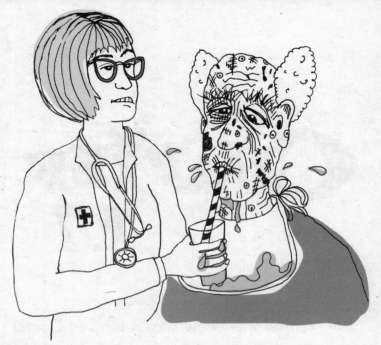

sure you want to proceed with the finals of the Crown Duels tomorrow, sire?"

He grunted grumpily.

"We could simply postpone the competition for a few weeks, until you feel better?" *And look better,* she thought.

"NO!" the king barked angrily. He grabbed a piece of paper and scribbled urgently. When he'd finished he thrust the handwritten note at her. She took it and read it out loud.

"It's difficult for me to speak because I swallowed some bees and they stung my throat, so here are my instructions. The contest will start at seven a.m. sharp tomorrow. I will write a welcome speech, but the prime minister will probably have to read it for me. The prime minister is to be warned that use of his fart machine AT ANY TIME will result in him being imprisoned for a month."

He snatched the paper back from her and scribbled something else.

Do I still smell slightly of poo? I can't tell any more…

"No, you smell lovely," Barbara lied. "Now try and drink some more of this smoothie, please, Your Majesty."

CHAPTER 18

Harry, his parents, his grandmother and Maddie and Cy sat in a circle on the floor of the living room. Jonathan had eventually come out of the bathroom, but he looked miserable.

"We could play that game where everyone says one word each and together we make a story? That might cheer us up," suggested their grandmother.

"If we do that, Cy will just say 'bumfuzzle' all the time," Maddie said, giving Cy a small shove.

"No, I won't!" retorted Cy. "And it's a real word anyway. It means confuse. So I can use it if I want."

"You just think it's funny to say 'bum'."

"No, I don't."

"Yes, you do."

"OK, fine. Whatever," interrupted Harry. "Let's play. You start, Cy."

Cy frowned in concentration. The rest of the family looked at him and waited.

"You just need to say one word," said Maddie after a moment.

"I know! I'm thinking!"

More frowning from Cy.

"Any word..."

"I'M THINKING!"

"OK, I'm not playing," said Maddie, and stood up.

"I'm not sure I'm up for it either," said

Jonathan, almost to himself.

"Oh, come on, Maddie," said Harry quickly. He couldn't bear it if the family wandered off and left his dad alone with his thoughts. He'd spent most of the day either in the bathroom or staring at the wall. "Let's play. Come on, Cy–"

"I've got one!" said Cy.

Maddie turned back. "Go on then," she said.

"Bumfuzzle!" Cy beamed.

"I'm going," said Maddie.

"No, don't. Please," urged Harry. "Please don't."

Harry looked beseechingly at her. He wanted her to understand that this was about something more important than a game. That it was about finding a way to be together after what had happened. It was about finding a way to fight off the despair they were all feeling.

"OK," she said, with a sigh. "Bumfuzzle it is. My word next?"

Harry nodded, grateful and relieved.

"Walked," said Maddie.

"Bumfuzzle walked? I thought 'bumfuzzle' was a verb?" asked their grandmother. She was lying flat on the floor of the sitting room. She said she had lost the ability to sit cross-legged about twenty-five years ago. Grandmother Sponge – or G-Sponge as Cy liked to call her – may have had trouble with her memory recently, she may have found much of what was happening to her bewildering, but the one thing she had never lost was a firm grasp on the rules of grammar. The rest of the family – who used to find it irritating to be constantly corrected – welcomed it as a sign that the woman they knew and loved hadn't disappeared completely and that the real G-Sponge was still in there somewhere. **"Saying 'bumfuzzle walked' is akin to saying, 'confuse walked',"** she continued.

"I'm using it as a proper noun," said Maddie. **"I think Bumfuzzle sounds like a character in an old-fashioned novel."**

"Ah, understood," said G-Sponge. **"Bumfuzzle is a person. Right. In that case ... Bumfuzzle walked..."**

Cy sat giggling. He couldn't believe his luck. Everyone was saying "bum" repeatedly.

"Backwards," said G-Sponge. "Bumfuzzle walked backwards. Your go, Hilary."

"Bumfuzzle walked backwards," repeated Harry's mum, Hilary.

Like Harry, she was very worried about Jonathan. The family had been all right while both parents had jobs – Hilary and Jonathan could keep up with the stream of bills that dropped relentlessly through the letter box. Then they'd borrowed a bit of money one December to get through the winter and buy the kids some presents. Then Hilary had broken her leg and couldn't work. And then Jonathan's company had got rid of lots of the staff. Eventually the people they'd borrowed the money from had wanted it back and they had no way to pay them. Hilary knew it wasn't Jonathan's fault, but she didn't know how to make *him* understand that.

"Bumfuzzle walked backwards towards," she said. "Your go, Jonathan."

"The," he said without looking up. Hilary took his hand.

"Bumfuzzle walked backwards towards the ... smelly," said Harry.

"OK, let's not repeat the whole thing every time," said Maddie. "Just say your word and quickly or we'll be here all day."

"All right, Boss Lady," said Cy sarcastically.

"Bumfuzzle walked backwards towards the smelly..." said Harry.

"I thought you weren't supposed to repeat the whole thing every time!"

"I'm just doing it one last time! Your go, Cy. Bumfuzzle walked backwards towards the smelly..."

"Smell."

"Which."

"He."

"Smelled."

"With."

"His."

"Smell."

"Machine."

"Which."

"Was."

"Called."

"BigSmell2000."

"Harry! That's four words!"

"No, BigSmell2000 is one word. Famous smell machine makers. Legendary. Your go, Cy. Start a new sentence."

Cy thought. "Bumfuzzle."

"For goodness' sake!"

"It's the name of our main character!"

"It's fine, Maddie," said Harry, trying to keep everyone on track. "Your go."

"Bumfuzzle knew."

"That."

"He."

"Had let everybody down," Jonathan said, getting up and walking out of the room.

CHAPTER 19

It was time for King Chisel to get some fresh air.

Normally he liked to walk in the palace gardens, but he was unable to walk today. He was still too battered and bruised. Instead, Doctor Face-Problem was going to wheel him around the gardens using a specially made trolley-throne built by Larry the gardener.

"Are you ready?" Barbara asked him. The king did his best to nod.

Larry the gardener had done a wonderful

job and the trolley glided effortlessly along. Barbara could push it with hardly any effort.

"This is lovely, isn't it?" Barbara exclaimed, as they passed under the Arch of Triumph towards the ornamental gardens at the rear of the palace.

The palace gardens were famous across the land. They had been designed by landscape architect Dame Suki Brown-Trousers over one hundred and fifty years before. There was one central path that ran from the palace in a straight line for over a kilometre down to the bottom fountains: twelve fountains in a circle that each shot water a hundred metres or so into air. The fountains were that powerful so that they could be clearly seen from the palace at the top of the hill, and they were called the bottom fountains because they were at the bottom of the hill, not because they had anything to do with bottoms.

On either side of the fantastically long path down to the bottom fountains were the most beautiful displays of flora imaginable. Thousands and thousands of gorgeous and rare plants cared for each day by an army of gardeners, under the watchful eye of the head gardener, Larry Bing-Bong.

(An interesting biographical detail about Larry: Larry's father, a travelling salesman called Ivor Bing-Bong, married Larry's mother, Sybil Bing. She wanted her child to keep her surname and suggested calling him Larry Bing-Bong-Bing or even Larry Bing-Bing-Bong, but Larry's dad thought that was silly. They argued about it until the day Sybil died after being crushed, ironically, by a grandfather clock that fell on her.)

The gardens were King Chisel's pride and joy. He never let a day go past without a stroll down the path to the bottom fountains. He believed that one of the reasons he had lived so long was due to the joy, serenity and happiness that the gardens brought him. He felt they made him a better, kinder and more tolerant person.

Larry Bing-Bong often suggested that it might be nice for the gardens to be open to the public every now and then, so that they too could experience this sense of calm, but King Chisel said, **"No. They're my gardens; everyone else can do one."**

Barbara Face-Problem pushed King Chisel's trolley to the top of the path and they both marvelled at the view. **"Every day this garden**

takes my breath away!" said the doctor. "Oh, wait! Sorry, I forgot your flask of tea. I'll be right back."

She ran back into the palace.

King Chisel looked out at his gardens. Despite all the various mishaps that had befallen him in the last few days, he felt pretty good. The finals of the Crown Duels were about to begin and soon he would have an heir. Then he'd be able to relax, knowing that the future of the monarchy was assured and his duty done.

As his throne slowly passed the white roses on the left and the red roses on the right, King Chisel reflected that he was a lucky man. He had lived a long and comfortable life, the sun was shining, the gardens were beautiful: things could be a lot worse. He passed the incredibly vivid tulips and then his favourite flowers – the lilies. He *loved* lilies. For him they symbolized innocence, purity and grace. They also reminded him of his mother, the late Queen Spanna. They were her favourite flowers and seeing them made King Chisel think fondly of her. As he glided past them his heart leapt with joy. He felt *good*. He felt *alive*. Almost happy. It was an unusual state of mind for him to be in, but he relished it.

Then a thought struck him – *I'm moving. Why am I moving?*

It was an intriguing thought and one to which he could not instantly find an answer. Barbara was still in the palace collecting his flask. Then it hit him. He was heading down the slope on his trolley because things on wheels will roll down slopes unless something is stopping them. Something like brakes.

This trolley contraption his throne was sitting on had no brakes.

King Chisel opened his mouth to scream for help, but no sound came out. The trolley, with its beautifully functioning wheels, moved faster and faster down the long slope. From behind him somewhere he could hear shouts – Barbara had returned and was calling for

help. But he was travelling so fast now that the main thing he could hear was the sound of wind rushing past his ears.

By the time King Chisel's trolley hit the wall of the fountain, he was travelling *fast*. The trolley stopped on impact but the king didn't. He sailed through the air and, just as he was about to land in the water, he was thrust skywards by one of the twelve high-powered jets of water of the bottom fountains.

As he fell back down towards the water, his mind was surprisingly calm given the circumstances. He thought about Barbara Face-Problem and Larry Bing-Bong and all the ways he was going to punish them once this ordeal was over.

CHAPTER 20

Honey knocked on Bernie's office door.

"WHAT?" came the grumpy response.

"It's Honey Plunge, Prime Minister."

"SO?"

"I'm here with the, ah, winner of the Breege County heat, Henrietta Musk."

"SO? ARE YOU TRYING TO BORE ME TO DEATH?"

"Well, there's a teensy, tiny problem that I'd like to run past you."

"A PROBLEM?"

The door flew open and Bernie, in a brown dressing gown and furry slippers, stuck his head out.

"**What's this all about?**" he asked grumpily. "**It's late.**"

"Oh, sorry. It's only six p.m., I thought..."

"I like to get into my jimjams at six p.m. and have a hot milk. Explain this problem."

Honey glanced at the girl who was standing beside her. She was a slim, tall figure with a curtain of long, straight dark brown hair brushed forward over her face.

"Tricky to, sir. Shall we go and discuss with the king?"

"No," said Bernie. "Come in. Let me hear what it is first."

"That's a little difficult..."

"GET INTO THIS ROOM, PLUNGE."

"Yes, sir. After you, Henrietta."

Henrietta Musk shuffled silently into Bernie's office followed by Honey. Bernie shut the door.

Two palace guards sat just inside the room. Due to an ancient tradition, palace guards

125

wore stuffed beavers on their heads instead of hats. The beavers were tied to their heads with string knotted underneath their chins; it was a tradition whose origins were lost in the mists of time. It was difficult for the guards to move without the beavers sliding off the tops of their heads, and running was all but impossible, but this was the way things had always been done, so this was the way they did it. Keeping their beavers in position was always the priority for the guards and they were under orders to attend to them before anything else.

"This is Henrietta Musk," said Honey to Bernie, **"the winner of the Breege heat today."**

Bernie inspected Henrietta. She didn't move a muscle. **"Whoop-de-doo,"** he said sarcastically. **"She looks like a mop on a stick. Go on."**

"Well," began Honey. Then she stopped.

"Look, sir, are you sure we shouldn't fetch the king?"

"Quite sure. Get on with it."

"Yes, sir. Well, Henrietta won the heat fair and square. But something about the way she was acting troubled me. For instance, I noticed that whenever her name was called, she didn't immediately react. Often we had to call her name several times to get her attention. Nothing too unusual, you might think; perhaps she's hard of hearing. I thought the same thing and was going to leave it at that, but I just couldn't. So I checked her medical records and found something remarkable. Henrietta Musk died fifty-two years ago!"

"Well, that is incredible!" said Farting Bernie. "She died fifty-two years ago! And she still managed to win her Crown Duels' heat!

Extraordinary! Well done you!" He patted Henrietta on the head.

"No, sir," said Honey, as gently as she could, "Henrietta didn't win her heat. She's been dead for fifty-two years."

"Which is what makes her achievement all the more remarkable!" continued Bernie. "Imagine winning when you're that dead! Brilliant!"

"The person who won today's heat was not Henrietta," continued Honey, speaking very slowly and clearly, "but an imposter. Someone pretending to be Henrietta. Stealing her identity."

"Oh," said Bernie.

Henrietta began to edge towards the door. "I looked into it," said Honey, "followed the paper trail, did some research, and I think I

128

know who this person is."

Suddenly Henrietta turned and bolted. The palace guards jumped towards her, but their beavers instantly slipped off the tops of their heads so they stopped to adjust them. However, Honey reached out a hand and grabbed "Henrietta" before she got any further.

"I can explain!" Henrietta said, her voice low and rasping. She reached up and pulled at her hair, which came off her head in one easy motion. Underneath was an elderly woman with short grey hair. **"My name is Lotus Forkleg,"** said the woman. **"I am a distant cousin of King Chisel, and I was disgusted when I heard that there was to be a competition to be the next monarch rather than giving the crown to one of the king's relatives. Like me. Just not fair! I wanted to be queen. I mean COME**

ON, how brilliant would that be? Henrietta was my grandmother and I miss her every day. I used her name to enter the competition. I'm so sorry for the trouble I've caused.

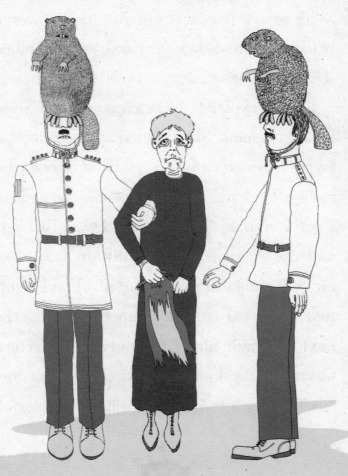

Any questions?"

"No questions, you're going to prison," said the prime minister, and signalled for the guards to remove Lotus Forkleg. This they did, pausing every few steps when their beavers needed readjusting. It took them nearly six minutes to shuffle out of the room. Meanwhile, Lotus Forkleg sang a mournful song that none of them had heard before – all about mountains, leaving home on boats and how green the grass was back where she came from – a song all of them earnestly hoped never to hear again.

"Right," said Honey once the cheat was gone. "I had better tell the king. He's going to be furious. The finals were supposed to start tomorrow morning and now we're missing a contestant."

"Wait!" said Bernie, frantically ruffling his

hair as he paced up and down. "Well, well, well. This is certainly an interesting situation. How can I turn it to my advantage?"

"I beg your pardon, sir?"

"Oh, did I say that out loud?" said Bernie. "I meant to say – how can we help fix this problem? Perhaps we can find a candidate to replace Lotus Frogslegs?"

"Forkleg."

"Whatever."

"We should really run the heat again," said Honey. "That's the fair and decent thing to do."

"And upset the king by not being ready to start tomorrow morning? Let's face it, Plunge, this mess is your doing and the king will not be pleased with you if he finds out."

"Me? But I was the one who uncovered

the imposter!"

"You allowed an eighty-four-year-old to enter a competition for children! I don't think King Chisel will be impressed to hear how badly you ran that heat, do you?"

"Being honest is the best policy," said Honey.

"Of course, of course," said Bernie, not very convincingly. "But let's think of His Majesty. Let's try and make life a little easier for him."

"How?"

"We find a replacement!" said Bernie. "Someone I can control!"

"Sir?"

"Oh, did I say that out loud too? Whoops. I meant to say we should choose someone gentle and kind and sort of soft. Know anybody?"

"Gentle, kind and sort of soft?"

"Yes, you know, someone who does what

they are told. Someone ... nice. Know anybody nice?"

"Well," said Honey, thinking back to earlier, "there was a boy..."

"Yes?"

"He was kind to me today when he didn't need to be."

"Go and get him! Tell him he's in the final of the Crown Duels and he's got me to thank!"

"But that's not fair on the others," objected Honey.

"We'll make it fair. I'll vet him myself before we start the finals, check he's worthy and all that, and then we'll treat him just like the others. Fair and square. So we can all be honest about everything blah blah blah. OK, got that? Bye!"

CHAPTER 21

Harry and Cy sat on the carpet in the living room, eating baked beans from the can. All their plates and cutlery had been taken so they were each using a cocktail stick to spear the beans one by one. Near them, sprawled on the floor, was their father. He had slept little for the last few nights, so Harry was pleased to see him getting some rest now. Maddie and their mum were out taking G-Sponge and Lemon for a walk.

BANG!

There was a
loud knock on the
door and Harry and Cy froze. The outside
world rarely came calling these days and when
it did it was always bad news.

Harry put his finger to his lips. Hopefully if
they stayed quiet whoever it was would think
no one was at home and go away.

They sat in silence for a few moments, scarcely daring to breathe. His father, muttering incomprehensibly to himself, slept on restlessly.

BANG! BANG! BANG!

Cy looked to Harry. Everyone always looked to Harry. Harry gestured that Cy should relax and that it would be fine.

They heard the letter box flap snap open and a man's voice shouted, **"HARRY SPONGE! OPEN UP! NOW!"**

Harry winced.

"SERIOUSLY! LET ME IN! IT'S GOOD NEWS, I PROMISE!" yelled the man through the letter box.

Harry shook his head at Cy. This was an old tactic. The men would pretend to be coming with good news and then once in through the

137

door they'd take … well, there was nothing left to take, so heaven knows what they'd do.

"HONEY PLUNGE SENT ME!"

That changed things. Honey Plunge? The woman from earlier? She had seemed like a decent person. Harry decided to take a chance. He opened the door.

"Hello. Can I ask you to whisper as I don't want to wake my father?" Harry whispered.

When he was told, in a whisper, that he'd been selected to be a finalist in the Crown Duels, Harry didn't believe it.

"It's true!" whispered the man, very quietly.

"But, how?" Harry whispered back. **"I didn't even get to enter the heats."**

"Yes," said the man, barely audibly, **"but you were selected by the prime minister himself on the advice of Miss Plunge. I promise you**

it's true! You need to report to the palace at six forty-five a.m. tomorrow morning."

Harry shook his head, totally bewildered. He pointed to himself. **"Me?"** he mouthed.

The man mouthed back, **"Yes, you."**

"Harry Sponge?"

The man thought his head was going to fall off if he kept nodding this vigorously.

"Really?" mouthed Harry.

"Yes!!!" mouthed the man, throwing in a double thumbs up to really ram the message home.

Harry and Cy looked at each other. They both shrugged, a smile creeping across their faces. Then Harry threw his arms in the air and, completely silently, he and Cy jumped up and down in celebration, punching the air with noiseless joy.

CHAPTER 22

The following morning, at seven o'clock, the five finalists for the Crown Duels were led into the Great Hall at the palace. They were told to sit on the stage in the seats with their names on. Facing them in the audience were rows and rows of dignitaries and special guests: the lady mayoress, the Chancellor of the Exchequer, the Lord Chancellor, the Keeper of the Rolls, the Archbishop, the Admiral of the Fleet and so on. Everybody who was anybody was there:

all the top academics, clergy, military, lawyers, doctors, business leaders and even a couple of the country's best writers, although they had to sit at the back near the toilets.

This, after all, was a hugely significant moment in the history of the country. On that stage sat their future king or queen. Which one of the five children it would turn out to be was about to be decided and the tension and excitement in the room was palpable.

The lady mayoress stood up and addressed the room. She was a short woman with an impressive nose. **"Oh, hello everyone! Welcome to this most thrilling of days. King Chisel has been slightly delayed after he was bitten by a goat this morning. I'm told he will be here shortly. Our prime minister should be here any minute..."**

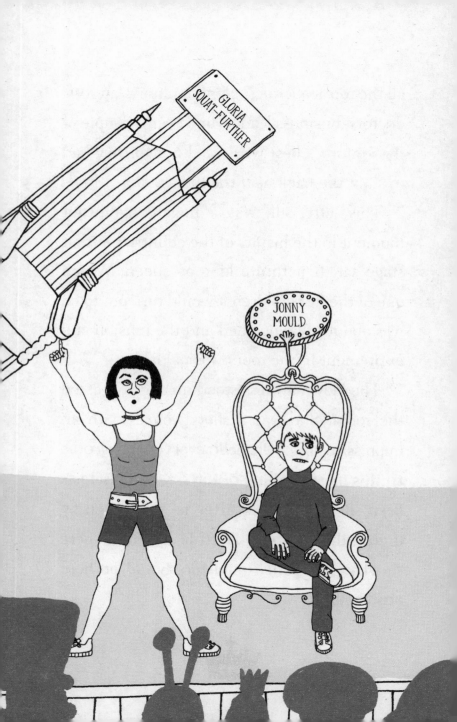

Everyone rolled their eyes. Farting Bernie thought it was fine to keep people waiting because he was special.

"So," continued the lady mayoress, "while we wait for the king, let us welcome our

HUXLEY BEELINE

GOSSAMER FOUNTAIN

HARRY SPONGE

finalists. Why don't the five of you introduce yourselves?" She sat down again and gestured to Gloria Squat-Further to go first.

Gloria stood up. "**Hello,**" she said confidently, "**my name is Gloria Squat-Further. I'm supremely fit and strong, both mentally and physically. I look forward to being your next queen.**" She threw her head back and let out a primal roar, beating her chest as she did. Then she jumped into a low crouch, threw a couple of karate kicks at thin air and somersaulted backwards, landing in the box splits. She stared at the other four children with ferocious intensity.

After a pause to make sure the girl had finished leaping about, the lady mayoress cried, "**Welcome, Gloria!**" and led the whole room in a warm and enthusiastic round of applause.

Gloria stood up, bowed, and returned to her seat.

"Hello," said the next child, neatly dressed in black trousers and a black turtleneck, "my name is Jonny Mould. I am an artist. Please don't ask me to be more specific. Art, and my art in particular, should be free to express itself in whatever medium feels most suitable. Sometimes I work with oil paints; sometimes with watercolours; sometimes with fruit; sometimes animation; sometimes live performance; or dance; or mime; or song and dance; or song and mime; or song and dance and mime; or song and dance and mime and fruit. The important thing is to create an emotional response in the viewer or listener or reader. I want you to feel something."

"I feel a bit confused!" shouted the Keeper

of the Rolls. **"Does that count?"**

The lady mayoress started a round of applause for Jonny Mould before things got out of hand.

The third child stood up. **"My name is Huxley Beeline,"** said Huxley Beeline, and sat down again. He felt that any further information at this point was superfluous. The room applauded politely.

Gossie stood up, her crystal pendants clanking together. **"My name is Gossamer Fountain, but most people call me Gossie. I'm most sensitive to feelings and ... aura. I've got to say, I'm getting quite an odd feeling from this room. Like bad things might have happened here, years ago. Like there are disturbed spirits floating around. Lost souls. Evil. A place of torture, perhaps. I smell pain.**

Nice curtains, though."

She sat down and everyone clapped uncertainly.

Harry, who was next, readied himself to speak. He had arrived at the palace early, as requested, and spoken privately to Bernie, which had been … confusing. For one thing, Bernie kept repeating, **"You owe me. You owe me. Remember that!"**

Harry was, of course, extremely grateful for the chance to compete in the finals and said he'd always remember the kindness Bernie and Honey had shown him.

"Not her!" Bernie had shouted. **"Just me! You owe everything to me! Got it?"**

Harry had never spoken to a prime minister before and thought maybe this was just what powerful men were like. So he'd nodded, which had seemed to satisfy Bernie.

Before Harry could get to his feet, though, a trumpet fanfare sounded and the doors at the back of the Great Hall burst open. Farting Bernie insisted on the trumpet fanfare. He hated the idea of entering a room unnoticed. Everyone fell silent and turned to look as he walked up the aisle.

Even though he was a popular figure with the general public because of his fart machine, the people that actually knew Bernie hated him. They knew what a mean, nasty, selfish liar he was. Bernie was fully aware of that. Still, he did his best to appear relaxed and happy, shaking hands with one or two of the dignitaries, playfully punching the Lord Chancellor on the arm, blowing the lady mayoress a kiss. This caused the lady mayoress to do a little bit of sick in her mouth.

Bernie trundled up to the stage, high-fived the children and then turned to acknowledge the crowd. **"Please, ladies and gentlemen!"** he called. **"That's enough clapping!"**

But everyone had already stopped clapping.

"Yes!" shouted Bernie. **"It's ME!"** And he unleashed a fart from his fart machine. He had been told of the king's threat to throw him in prison for using it, but the king hadn't arrived yet and if anyone told on him he'd just lie and say, **"Who are you going to believe, them or the prime minister?"** No one laughed at the fart noise and Bernie sat down, a little red in the face.

Then the king entered.

A gasp went up from the back of the Great Hall. The king looked *dreadful*. His face was a mess. His lips were hugely swollen from the bee stings, his left eye had closed almost completely, his right was severely bruised, he had a splint across his nose, his scalp was a sea of scabs and several of his teeth were missing. He was covered in scratches too.

The five contestants were astonished. This was *not* how they'd thought the king would look. Huxley wondered for a moment whether trying to become king was worth it if this was what it did to a person.

King Chisel was wheeled in on the throne-trolley, which was being pushed by Honey. The king had had a bad morning. He had insisted on being pushed to the stables to visit his horse. However, because his eyes were so swollen, he couldn't see very well and instead of his horse, Señor Legs, he had patted a goat,

150

Rodney Dangertubes.

Rodney Dangertubes was a grumpy goat at the best of times, but that morning he was feeling especially tetchy and when His Majesty tickled him under the

chin and called him a "good boy" Rodney didn't react well. He bit the king hard on the arm.

Honey pushed King Chisel up the aisle as the audience stood respectfully. They stared in horror at the king. Since the accident with the fountain yesterday, the wheels on the trolley squeaked loudly and tended to veer to the left. This meant that every few rows the throne would smash painfully into an audience member before Honey could correct its course.

SQUEAK, SQUEAK, SQUEAK.

"OW!"

"Sorry!"

SQUEAK, SQUEAK, SQUEAK.

"OW!"

"Sorry!"

SQUEAK, SQUEAK, SQUEAK.

"OW!"

"Sorry!"

Once at the stage, Honey realized it would be tricky to get the king up on to it. There was a flight of stairs to negotiate. She looked pleadingly at the dignitaries in the front row and four of them joined her to lift the trolley and, on it, the throne containing the silent king. Silent only because his mouth was too swollen for him to speak. Inside, he was seething at the indignity of all this. *Haven't you ever seen a man who's fallen downstairs, been stung a thousand times, had his head ripped to pieces by a cat, smashed into a fountain and been bitten by an angry goat before?!?* he wanted to yell at the gawkers.

Honey, the Admiral of the Fleet, the Lord Chancellor, Gregory Plumsocket and Sister Metallica volunteered to lift him on to the stage. Unfortunately, just as they reached the top step, Gregory Plumsocket's bad back twinged and spasmed and he let go. The trolley tilted, the throne slid off and the king fell through the air, landing nose first on to the stone floor of the Great Hall.

"Doctor Face-Problem!" shouted Honey. **"We need you! Again!"**

CHAPTER 23

With the king patched up as much as possible, the ceremony could begin.

Bernie stood up and walked to the front of the stage, with the king's speech stuffed into his pocket.

"Gosh! Wowzers! Look at you all!" he blustered. Everyone in the room stared back at him with contempt. **"I bet you didn't expect to hear from me, your prime minister, but our glorious king is a little under the weather**

at the moment." He turned to King Chisel, who grimaced and softly spat out a tooth. "**So it gives me great pleasure to read out his introductory speech to this great event.**"

Farting Bernie unfolded the speech and started to read.

"*Hello. This is your king. Let's get on with it. The prime minister, Smitherington-Piffle, will read this. Beyond reading this letter don't assume that he speaks for me in any way. The man is a complete berk. I mean look at him. Listen to that voice. He has absolutely nothing to recommend him. What a pillock! I hate him.*"

Farting Bernie chuckled as best he could. "**Remember what a terrific sense of humour our king has,**" he said. "**He's a real joker.**" He continued: "*Welcome to the five chosen*

children. Congratulations. You are the best
your counties have to offer. Over the next
few days you will be put through a series of
tests and challenges, and then one of you will
be chosen to be the next king or queen.

"There are rules. Listen carefully. You may
be asked to leave at any time. If you are, go.
It's over for you. You are not to help each
other at any point. You are to work alone. Any
assistance given to another contestant will
result in instant disqualification. No cheating.
No whinging. Oh, and good luck."

The prime minister lowered the piece of
paper. "Thank you, Your Royal Highness. Now
the five contestants will be taken to the Hall
of Mirrors, where the contest will begin, a
series of testing, er, tests set by our king. Let
us cheer them on their way. So, step forward:

Gloria Squat-Further!"

The crowd started to applaud.

"Jonny Mould! Huxley Beeline! Gossamer Fountain! And the final entrant," said Bernie, "from Breege County, a lovely lad that I think has tremendous promise, Harry Sponge!! Any final words of encouragement, Your Majesty?"

They looked to King Chisel. He'd fallen into a deep, deep sleep.

CHAPTER 24

"Right," said Farting Bernie. "I'm in charge here. I'm the prime minister and I'm in charge. OK?"

Farting Bernie, Honey Plunge and Doctor Barbara Face-Problem were holding a crisis meeting in the prime minister's office. They had not been able to rouse the king and, in the end, they'd had to put him to bed. He had been through an awful lot in the last few days.

This, however, presented a problem as far

as the Crown Duels were concerned. The king was supposed to set the contestants a series of tasks. And he was dead to the world.

"How about we wait for the king to have a nice sleep and begin the Crown Duels once he wakes up?" suggested Honey.

"I'm in charge, didn't you catch that part?" said Bernie. "I'll make the decisions. Doctor, sleep is good for the king, right?"

"Absolutely."

"Then this is what we're going to do," said Bernie. "We will lock the king in his bedroom..."

"But..."

"I'M IN CHARGE!! QUIET! Put him in his room so that he can get a massively long sleep because the longer he sleeps the better, and in the meantime I'll set the tasks for the Crown Duels, any questions? No? Good! Let's go! I'M

IN CHARGE!"

Bernie swept out of the room. Barbara and Honey looked at each other uneasily.

"Who's in charge again?" joked Barbara, but Honey was too worried to smile.

CHAPTER 25

The five Crown Duels contestants were gathered in the Hall of Mirrors.

This was perhaps the most famous room in the palace. Designed seventy years earlier by the architect Sir Philip Droppings, it consisted of over three hundred mirrors, hung along every side of the long narrow room. Etched on each mirror were drawings by great artists, mostly scenes from history or notable persons or pictures of well-known beauty spots. It was considered a national treasure. Every young child in the country knew of the Hall of Mirrors.

Unfortunately, over the last fifty years, King Chisel had more or less destroyed it. He used the hall as a shortcut to get from his office to the dining room, and had either stumbled, tripped or staggered into every single mirror. Most were cracked; others were completely shattered. Only one had survived intact.

Huxley Beeline gasped as he took it all in. **"The Hall of Mirrors! Who did this?"**

"Breaking one mirror is seven years of bad luck," said Gossie. **"Whoever did this will be unlucky for about eight thousand years!"**

"When I win," Gloria said, **"the first thing I'm going to do is restore this room to its rightful glory."**

"**When** you win?" Jonny interrupted. "You mean *if* you win?"

"No," said Gloria, walking over to Jonny so that they were standing toe to toe. She was quite a bit taller than him and stared down at him unblinking. "**I'm going to win, Art Boy, and you and your fruit-based whatevers better get used to it. Ya get me?**"

"'Ya get me'?" said Huxley Beeline, frowning. "Don't you mean 'Do you understand me'? 'Ya get me' is inelegant."

"You know what will be inelegant?" asked Gloria, whipping round to face Huxley Beeline. "**When you cry so hard after being beaten by me in this competition that you get washed away on a river of your own tears. That'll be inelegant, sunshine.**"

Farting Bernie strolled into the hall,

followed by Honey Plunge and Doctor Barbara.

"Welcome one and all. I'm the prime minister!" He paused here for a round of applause, but one didn't materialize so he continued. "I guess you all knew that. This is it, everyone. The start of the competition. This is where things get serious."

Bernie smiled and did what he always did when lost for words – pressed the button on the fart machine. The fart it produced was so quiet it could barely be heard. The batteries in the machine were running low. However, the small sad little *pfft* it emitted gave him an idea.

"Yes! That's it!" he exclaimed. "Your first trial, contestants, is to create the Best Sound. Yes, there we go. That'll do. Create a sound.

The best one wins the round."

Huxley Beeline opened his mouth to ask a question, but Farting Bernie cut him off.

"The Best Sound. You have one hour. GO!"

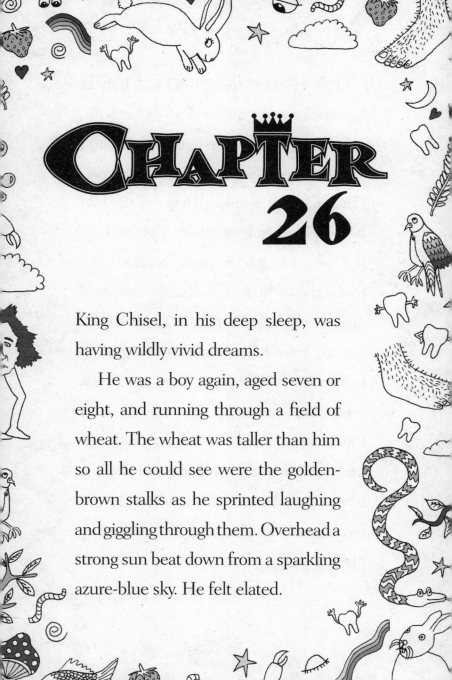

CHAPTER 26

King Chisel, in his deep sleep, was having wildly vivid dreams.

He was a boy again, aged seven or eight, and running through a field of wheat. The wheat was taller than him so all he could see were the golden-brown stalks as he sprinted laughing and giggling through them. Overhead a strong sun beat down from a sparkling azure-blue sky. He felt elated.

The wheat parted in front of him as he ran, creating a corridor – a smooth, soft, wide corridor. He looked down and saw that he was running on red carpet. He looked up and saw that the sky had become darker, grey clouds passing over the sun. He stopped. He reached out to touch a wheat stalk, but it remained just out of his grasp. He ran again, wildly, veering from left to right, trying to grab something solid, something real, but everything remained too far away to touch. He became increasingly agitated and distraught, swerving, swooping, lurching – the wheat out of reach, the red carpet underfoot and overhead a sky quickly turning blacker.

CHAPTER 27

It had been almost an hour since Bernie set the task. Their time was nearly up.

Jonny Mould, who had changed into a black leotard and jazz shoes, sat on a yoga mat in the centre of the Hall of Mirrors, going through a series of stretches.

Gloria Squat-Further kicked open the door. **"Wassup, you spanner?"** she bellowed at him.

Jonny ignored her and concentrated on taking deep breaths.

Gossie and Huxley joined them. "We're not late, are we?" Gossie asked anxiously.

Huxley checked his watch. "We're twelve seconds early."

"My sound is amazing," said Gloria. "This first round is in the bag and once I get a lead I never let it go."

Harry slipped into the hall. He gave them all a half-smile, but Jonny was the only one who smiled back. Gossie ignored him. Huxley was lost in thought. Gloria Squat-Further gave him her most menacing stare. A stare that tried to say,

"Give up now, loser. You have no chance."
She put so much effort into this stare that she
emitted a low moan.

"Do you need the toilet?" Gossie asked her.

"What?!" said Gloria. "No!"

Harry had spent the whole hour hiding
behind a wall in the palace garden, desperately
trying to think of a sound. He was so nervous
his mind had gone completely blank. The
harder he tried to think of something, the
blanker his mind had become. Then panic
had set in. He was going to blow it in the first
round. He had no idea what he was going
to do.

Farting Bernie, Honey Plunge, the doctor
and some guards came in and sat down.

"Time's up," said Bernie. "Let's hear what

you've got. Why don't you kick things off, Humphrey Bedstain?"

"Huxley Beeline," said Honey.

"Whatever."

Huxley walked forward to the long wooden table, carrying a glass bowl full of murky water. He put it down and turned to face Honey and Farting Bernie. Behind them sat a row of guards, all sitting as upright as possible to maintain the vertical integrity of their beavers.

Huxley took in his audience, then pressed the tips of his fingers together. "The oceans," he began, "are big. Vast. Huge. They contain many wonders. When it comes to sound, however, one creature produces something simply astonishing. You might have heard that blue whales are big and produce a big sound. The loudest of any creature on earth, some believe. A sound that can be heard a thousand miles away. Impressive, certainly. But there is a sea creature that is louder." He paused, then his brow furrowed. "At least in terms of decibels. You might be familiar with decibels; they are a measurement of sound. Just one measurement, though. In fact, there are many ways to measure sound – STOP IT, HUXLEY! Where was I? Let me start again. Sorry."

Huxley turned away to compose himself. He was feeling the pressure of the occasion in a way that he hadn't expected. He took a couple of deep breaths and began again.

"Forgive me," he said. "I will recommence. Yes, there is a sea creature that is LOUDER than a blue whale! YES! What is this creature? Is it as big as a blue whale perhaps? Remember, a blue whale can grow to be longer even than this Hall of Mirrors – they are massive. Take forty paces and that's the length of a blue whale. The blue whale has a tongue that weighs the same as a fully grown elephant. Is this creature of which I speak as big as that? NO! This creature is so much smaller! This creature is about as long as your little finger and yet produces a noise, a sound, that is louder than that of a blue whale."

Huxley knew he was talking too much, but he couldn't stop himself. He placed his hands on either side of the glass bowl. "The creature to which I refer is the pistol shrimp and it produces a noise that can kill! That does kill! That has killed! That will kill again!"

He looked at the other contestants. Harry nodded encouragingly but he thought he saw Gossie suppressing a yawn. *Get on with it,*

Huxley thought, *I'm boring them.* He forced a laugh. *Why am I laughing? Now I look unhinged!*

"How can a noise kill? Let me tell you. One of the pistol shrimp's claws grows to half the size of its body. When it opens the claw, water rushes into the little elbow space created, then they slam the claw shut with such mind-boggling force that water shoots out at incredible speed, creating a powerful bubble that kills whatever is in its path! Wow! The sound made when the bubble bursts is louder than a gun going off, louder than the song of a blue whale. The bubble is hotter than lava from a volcano! In fact, it's four times hotter than lava!" He took a deep breath and wiped his brow. "So there we have it. My entry for Best Sound is the incredible sound of the awesome pistol shrimp. Thank you."

Huxley Beeline picked up his glass bowl, bowed and walked back to his seat. The others gave him a polite round of applause.

"**Well done, Huxley,**" said Honey warmly. "**Fascinating. May we hear the pistol shrimp making its sound?**" She laughed. "**If it's not too dangerous, that is!**"

"No," said Huxley. "**I don't have a pistol shrimp here.**"

"**Oh,**" said Honey. "**Isn't there one in the bowl?**"

"No."

"**Oh. Then why did you have the bowl with you?**"

"**To create a sense of mystery?**" Huxley smiled weakly and pushed his glasses up his nose.

"I see," said Honey. "Thank you. Anything to add, Prime Minister?"

She turned to Bernie, but he'd fallen asleep.

Huxley blinked twice. He was at a loss. When his father had died, the world had suddenly stopped making sense. It was a confusing, messy, awful place. For him, trying to understand the world, learning how it worked: the physics, the maths, the geography, everything; learning about people and animals and plants and the planet; gathering *information* and *knowledge* was not only fascinating but *important*. It helped him to banish that chaos. To give everything some order where there suddenly was none. And the pistol shrimp was a great example, he thought, of how magical and strange and surprising the world could be and of how much there was out there to admire and discover and enquire about.

And the prime minister had been so bored by it all that he'd fallen asleep.

Huxley thought about his mother, waiting anxiously at home to hear how it all went. He couldn't go home and tell her he had bored the prime minister so much he'd sent him to sleep! She'd be devastated.

"Well, I thought that was absolutely fascinating," said Honey gently. **"Next up is Gossie."**

CHAPTER 28

King Chisel slept on.

The sky had now turned completely black and in his dream, seven-year-old King Chisel stood motionless. Alone in total darkness, he could see nothing. All he could hear was the sound of his own breathing and the rapid beating of his heart. He tried to call out for his mummy, but no words came. He stepped forward and fell, soundlessly, effortlessly, down and down and down through space.

CHAPTER 29

Gossie stood. Silently, with a half-smile, she took them in one by one, occasionally nodding to herself, as if she was gathering important information. After some time, she pointed at Farting Bernie, still asleep, and said, **"Yes, you. I think you. Please come forward, Prime Minister."**

Honey shook Bernie awake. Disorientated, he blearily opened his eyes. **"Time to butter your crumpets, Headmaster?"** he said.

"It's the Crown Duels, Prime Minister," Honey told him. **"Gossie would like you to join her over there."**

"Gotcha. Gotcha. Gotcha," Bernie mumbled. He got up and staggered over to Gossie. She produced two thick woollen rugs and laid them carefully on the large wooden table.

"Please, Prime Minister, hop up on to the table and lie down."

"You're not going to saw me in half or anything, are you?" asked Farting Bernie.

"Oh, no!" Gossie laughed. **"Nothing so basic. Please."**

Farting Bernie, with quite a bit of effort, got on to the table and lay down.

"Are you comfortable?" asked Gossie.

"Yup."

"Good. Then I'll begin. I am going to guide

181

you through an exploration of your past lives."

"My what?"

"Your past lives. All of us have lived many lives before this one, of course. Some part of your previous lives is carried forward from one to the next. For instance, something awful might have happened to you when you were living one of your past lives and that emotional damage will be buried inside you."

"But I've only had one life. I've always been

a politician. Unless you mean like when I was a teenager and I used to burn Daddy's money in front of poor people for fun?" Everyone winced at this, but Bernie giggled at the memory.

"No, I mean entirely different lives, hundreds of years ago," said Gossie. "I can guide you through them."

"Goodness. This I want to see."

"Thank you, Prime Minister," said Gossie, slightly regretting that she'd chosen Bernie as her subject. She'd thought he would be flattered to be chosen. "I want you to relax. Close your eyes. Imagine you are lying on a hot sandy beach. The waves of the sea are lapping gently at the shore. The sun is warm. The sand is warm. Your body sinks into it. Let your legs feel heavy. Let your arms feel heavy. Let your head feel heavy. Relax your jaw. Breathe in. Breathe out. Breathe in. Breathe out. Listen to the sea."

"Can I go for a splashy splashy splash splash?" asked Bernie, eyes still closed.

"Please don't speak. Surrender to the experience. Just breathe. You are relaxed and you are safe and you are moving backwards in time. Back through the years, back through the centuries to another life."

"Yes," said Bernie faintly.

"What do you see?"

"I see grass," Bernie mumbled.

"Grass? Good. Are you standing on this grass?"

"I'm eating it. It's yummy."

"You're eating it? Right, good, grass, eating it. This is good. We've found a past life. What else?"

"Someone's coming over. Someone smaller than me."

"Who is it?"

"I can't see. They have a big tongue."

"Interesting."

"There's a lot of spit falling out of their mouth."

"Really?"

"Now they're..."

"Yes?"

"They ... my udder."

"Your udder?"

"Yup."

"You're a cow?"

"*MOOOOOOOOO.*"

Gossie turned to Honey, the doctor and the other contestants. **"And that's my sound,"** she said.

185

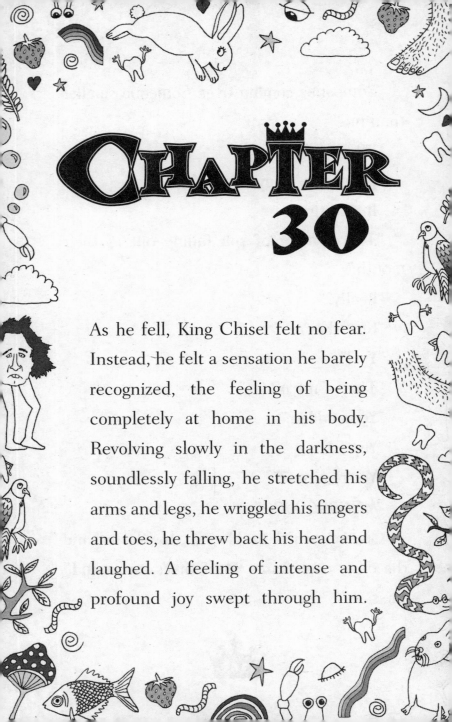

CHAPTER 30

As he fell, King Chisel felt no fear. Instead, he felt a sensation he barely recognized, the feeling of being completely at home in his body. Revolving slowly in the darkness, soundlessly falling, he stretched his arms and legs, he wriggled his fingers and toes, he threw back his head and laughed. A feeling of intense and profound joy swept through him.

He felt whole; he felt complete. For perhaps the first time since his wife died, he felt *happy*.

CHAPTER 31

Gloria Squat-Further chalked her palms, smashed her hands together, sending clouds of dust into the air, and settled in front of the huge barbell.

"This is the heaviest weight ever attempted by a girl my age," she said. "If I lift this, I will have done something no one my age has ever done before in the history of the human race. The sounds that I produce in making this attempt will be, if I succeed, the Best Sounds because they will have been responsible for making history. How many sounds can make that claim?"

The weight was so heavy it had taken all the contestants and three guards to lift it into place.

"I will now go deep within myself to produce an act of superhuman strength. Listen hard."

Gloria began to breathe in and out rapidly. She slapped her thighs, then her shoulders, spread her arms wide and screamed, **"BATTER MY BISCUITS!"** She placed her hands on the barbell and began to pull hard, yelling, **"GIVE ME A SPAM FRITTER, BABYSITTER!"** before unleashing the most gut-wrenching, soul-shredding yowl of her life. She lifted the weight up over her head, straightened her shaking arms … and, slowly, like a mighty tree felled in a forest, toppled backwards, smashing on to the hard wooden surface, the barbell breaking three floorboards.

There was a moment of stunned silence.

"Which one of those noises was her sound?" asked Bernie.

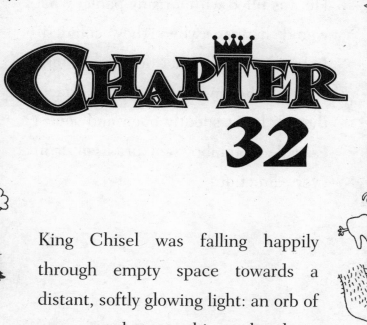

CHAPTER 32

King Chisel was falling happily through empty space towards a distant, softly glowing light: an orb of some sort that grew bigger the closer he got. He suddenly understood that the distances involved were enormous and that the globe itself was the size of a planet. The glare it gave off was becoming uncomfortable to look at and King Chisel shielded his eyes.

He was filled with a rising panic: what would happen when they collided? Before he could react or think or take a breath, he smashed into the surface, the orb burst silently open and sent a cascade of rainbow-coloured glitter in every direction.

CHAPTER 33

Jonny Mould tried to clear his mind of thought, but it wasn't easy. He sat cross-legged on the table, imagining a thread coming out of the top of his head being gently pulled upwards to help lengthen and straighten his spine.

Jonny had always felt like he saw the world in a different way to most other people. And certainly in a different way to his parents. Jonny found mystery exciting and plain facts dull.

A fact just lies there. It's shallow. It has no movement. It doesn't call out to you. But mystery ... wow ... into the unknown, *that* was true excitement! His mum and dad could not get that. If they saw something new or something they didn't immediately understand they grew fearful and anxious. They needed certainty and order and familiarity. Jonny found this tedious. He felt like a stranger in his own house and often wondered if maybe he'd been adopted and no one had told him, or he was from another planet, or this whole life was just a dream being dreamed by a powerful and strange being.

Nothing was real. Nothing would last. That was the sort of thing he loved and wanted more of. Not **"have you cleaned your room?"** or **"have you brushed your teeth?"**

As soon as Jonny had heard about the Crown Duels, he knew he had to enter. Transforming from ordinary child into a king? Journeys into the unknown don't get any bigger than that! So much to explore and experience – power, fame, wealth. So much to lift him out and away from his dull, ordinary world and into a fairy-tale fantasy!

He took in a slow, measured breath. He held it for a fraction and then released it with a sigh.

"**The breath of life,**" he explained to his audience softly. "**The breath of a child, of a mother, of a frightened wolf, of a newborn puppy. The breath of our dreams, of all our yesterdays and all our tomorrows. The breath which nourishes and protects and serves us. We are the breath and the breath is us. The**

Breath. The Sound. Thank you."

Getting back up, he walked to his chair and sat down, thinking as he did that it had gone pretty well, all things considered. The other children nodded politely, except Gloria, whose face was scrunched up in confusion. Then Jonny overheard Farting Bernie whispering to Honey, **"What a twenty-four-carat weirdo!"**

CHAPTER 34

As the glitter vanished, King Chisel saw that he was now wearing a pair of rainbow-coloured baggy dungarees with a white rope belt, a pink velvet beret and had a parrot on each shoulder. He reminded himself that this was a dream and not real. Out of the darkness, spinning gently, a strawberry milkshake spun into view.

The king grabbed it with a gloved hand and noisily took a slurp. It tasted of feet – and not in a good way. He spat it out, except it wasn't liquid that came out of his mouth but a rabbit.

"Hello!" said the bunny. "My name is Brendan. Brush me!"

This dream is getting pretty weird, thought the king.

CHAPTER 35

It was Harry's turn. He got up and walked to the table. He'd been thinking hard while the others had demonstrated their Best Sounds. What was his Best Sound, his favourite sound in all the world? He knew the answer to that. But was it unusual or profound enough compared to the sound of a killer shrimp, a past life, a record being broken, or the breath of life?

"Ah! I'm looking forward to this fellow!"

said Bernie as Harry nervously took his place. "He looks like he's got what it takes, don't you think?"

"I think it's far too early to say," said Honey, shooting him a look that said, *remember we promised to be fair and honest.*

"Of course, of course," said Bernie. "Too early to say." Then he winked.

"Hi, I'm Harry," Harry said. "My Best Sound is the sound of my dog, Lemon, licking my face when he hasn't seen me for a bit. He gets overexcited and he jumps up and licks my face and it's such a great sound. It reminds me of all the funny, silly things in life and how great it is to be loved. And I know you'd like to hear it and Lemon isn't here, so I guess I'm just going to have to..."

Harry hesitated, then brought his left

hand up and licked the back of it in the best
impersonation of Lemon he could manage.
He did this for several seconds before
feeling a bit silly. He stopped.

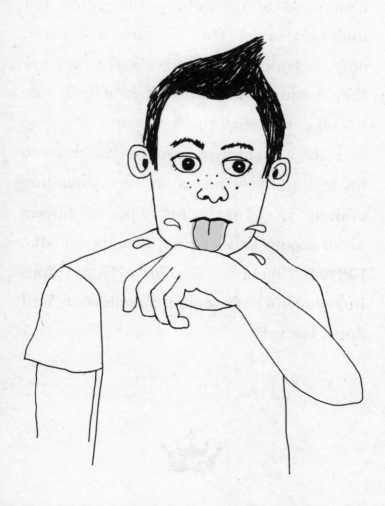

Then he went back to his chair and sat down.

Everyone was silent. A feeling of doom swept over him. Had he already blown it? Compared to the others, his sound felt underwhelming. This was the one – the only – chance the Sponges had to reverse their fortunes and he hadn't even been able to make it through the first round.

So he was surprised when Bernie leapt to his feet and gave him a prolonged standing ovation. The prime minister put his fingers in his mouth and let out a piercing whistle. **"WOW!"** shouted Bernie. **"That. Was. Incredible. What a sound! Magnificent. Well done, Harry!"**

CHAPTER 36

Meanwhile, in King Chisel's dream, Brendan the bunny and an orchestra of ninety purple rabbits were playing "Happy Birthday" to a goldfish.

This, thought King Chisel, *is getting ridiculous now.*

His hair had turned into snakes, his legs had become a fish's tail, he wore a spangly orange tube top, his hands were crab claws and he lay on a chaise longue surrounded by a sea of Farting Bernie heads that were walking around on little legs where their necks should be.

What next? he thought. *Singing cabbages? A leopard called Dylan with a lisp? An exploding swimming pool full of armpit hair?*

He looked up. It was raining teeth.

CHAPTER 37

Harry, Gloria, Gossie, Huxley and Jonny sat together at the far end of the Hall of Mirrors. They had been there for thirty minutes. They looked down the other end of the room, where Honey and Farting Bernie were talking animatedly.

"**What are they talking about, do you think?**" asked Jonny.

"I suspect," answered Huxley, "**that they are arguing about who presented the Best Sound.**"

"Me!" said Gloria. "I had the Best Sound! The sound of triumph."

"It wasn't a triumph!" retorted Gossie. "You fell over!"

Harry watched Honey and the prime minister. Honey looked flustered; Bernie looked angry.

Gloria got bored of waiting and started doing press-ups.

"OK!" Bernie yelled at them from the other end of the room. "COME HERE, YOU LOT! HURRY!"

The five contestants ran back to their chairs and sat. Honey Plunge, red in the face and breathing heavily, looked down at her lap. Farting Bernie clapped his hands together a couple of times.

"Hurry up and sit down!"

206

They were already sitting down.

"Right," he continued, "all good here. Honey Plunge and I are completely in agreement on everything, not that it matters because I'M IN CHARGE. So, this is what is going to happen, and I don't care if a certain somebody doesn't like it or thinks it's not the right way to run a competition as important as this or that it doesn't make sense. Let's get on to Round Two, shall we? Which is going to be all about ME." The kids stared at him and he laughed. "That's right! You all have one hour to come up with a poem or a song or a dance or anything really but it has to be about ME. And why I'm so great. Thank you. Goodbye."

Farting Bernie stood, but Honey reached out and took his arm.

"What?" he snapped. She whispered in his ear. "Oh." He sat back down again. "I've realized that

I haven't told you the results of Round One. I realized that all on my own. No one told me. So here we go..."

He looked at the five contestants and frowned.

"In last place is ... um ... you," he said, jabbing a finger towards Jonny. "Your weird breathing thing was ... well, look, we all breathe so it felt a bit 'so what'. Fourth place is you, Gloria, because it was a good effort but you fell over, and a queen shouldn't fall over, but I did once have a babysitter and she did give me a spam fritter which was delicious so well done for that so I've changed my mind, you're second. Boy with a dirty bowl is third. I'm afraid I MAY have fallen asleep, and a king shouldn't be boring, and the girl who made me moo is fourth." He shot Gossie a dirty look. "Queens shouldn't make prime ministers moo. And Harry wins, obviously. His sound was wonderful. Moving, dramatic, historic, which is everything a king should be. All clear? Good. BYE."

And he left. The guards ran to follow him out and all their beavers fell off.

Honey Plunge looked round at Harry, Gossie, Gloria, Huxley and Jonny. Gossie in particular looked furious.

"**Well**," Honey said quietly. "**Here we are. I think it might be useful to recap on the standings after Round One in case that was ... unclear. As things stand: Harry is first, Gloria second, then Huxley, Gossie and Jonny is currently last.**"

Huxley raised his hand. "**I have questions**," he said.

Honey sighed. "**I'm sure you do. I might not be able to answer them but please fire away.**"

"**What is the scoring system?**" asked Huxley.

"How many rounds will there be? Will the prime minister be judging all the rounds like that, or will there be more stringent criteria in place? Are we all going to be here until the end, or will contestants be asked to leave as we go along?"

"Yes," replied Honey, "all good questions and, believe me, questions I would love to know the answers to myself. All I can say is that you should try your very best and hope the king wakes up soon."

"He only put me in second-last place because I discovered he was a cow in a former life – that seems wrong," said Gossie. "He should thank me." She kicked the wall. Hard. This startled Harry. He didn't have Gossie down as super-ambitious or competitive.

"That's sour grapes," said Gloria. "I think the

ruling was fair. Second place after Round One, just where I wanted to be."

"You've changed your tune," said Jonny. "You said you'd win the first round!"

Gloria laughed. "And you believed me? That's good. I'm getting in your head. Got you exactly where I want you."

Harry was chewing his lip. This was making him feel uneasy. Of course he felt lucky to be in the lead – but he didn't think he deserved to be. He couldn't understand why Bernie was being so nice to him.

"I'll try to clarify the rules," said Honey. "I promise I'll do my best. Congratulations to Harry on leading the way. Good luck to you all with the next task. See you in an hour."

CHAPTER 38

King Chisel tried to ignore the pink giant sitting beside him. It must have been three times taller than the king and made entirely of marshmallow.

"Hello," it said to King Chisel. "Did you come for tea?"

CHAPTER 39

"Are you sure you don't want to change into proper gym clothes for your session, Prime Minister?" asked Randolph LaTouche.

"What do you mean? I look terrific!" said the prime minister.

Randolph wasn't so sure. Bernie had taken his tie and suit jacket off and rolled up his trousers, revealing black socks pulled up over chunky white calves. He still had a pair of black leather shoes on. He'd rolled up the sleeves of his white shirt and undone the top three buttons, revealing more of his pasty white chest than Randolph was entirely comfortable with.

While the contestants were composing poems and songs in his honour, Bernie had decided to pop along and see the king's personal trainer. Maybe it was time he got fit too.

"You might be more at ease in traditional gym wear, Prime Minister," Randolph suggested tartly. He himself was kitted out in a lilac leotard, yellow legwarmers, white jazz pumps and a white headband – his favourite outfit.

"Just pass me Jermaine, LaTouche," said the prime minister. **"Let's get on with it."**

Randolph hesitated. Jermaine was a large beaver and might be too heavy for Bernie. But

he needn't have worried. The prime minister was built like a small brick building and was extremely strong.

Bernie lay back on the bench, and holding Jermaine with both hands, thrust him up and down.

"You might want to come and watch Round Two of the Crown Duels, LaTouche," panted Bernie. "Going to be great fun. Got them writing about me! How about that!"

"How about that," repeated Randolph. "That's rather brave of you."

"Brave?" snorted Bernie. "What do you mean?"

"Well, sometimes children can be delightfully ... honest. They can be rather direct. Some of them have yet to learn the art of tact. I was once told by the young daughter of a friend of mine that I have the face of a worried horse. Still bothers me."

"Nonsense!" said Bernie again. "You're wrong and I'll tell you why. Pass me Sonia – I want to work on my triceps."

Randolph took Jermaine back from Bernie and scooped up Sonia the coyote – carefully, as Sonia had been asleep and could be grumpy if woken suddenly.

"Firstly, I was very clear that they have to say what they *like* about me. Secondly, there's nothing bad to say about me. Nothing at all. Thirdly, if they're stupid enough to speak ill of me, they'll find themselves out of the competition before they can blink. I don't want a king or queen who thinks for themselves – I want one who does what they're told. By me. Understand?"

LaTouche smiled tightly.

"So if any of those candidates are stupid enough to say anything bad about me I will destroy them. It's that simple." Bernie threw Sonia at Randolph, leapt off the bench, his shirt drenched in sweat, grabbed his tie and jacket and headed for the door.

"Wouldn't you like a shower before getting dressed, Prime Minister?" asked Randolph, but the prime minister was already gone.

CHAPTER 40

Farting Bernie, shirt stuck to his damp torso, bounced into the Hall of Mirrors.

"I'm here. Let's go," he said.

Honey and the contestants had agreed they should go in the reverse order from the previous round, which meant Harry was up first.

"Remember," shouted Bernie, "what it is you most like about me. Go!"

He took his seat next to Honey, who edged

her chair slightly away. Behind them sat the doctor and, slipping in through the door at the last minute, Randolph LaTouche.

Harry jumped up and stood in front of the assembled group. Bernie applauded loudly.

"I wrote some limericks," Harry said, **"to express my feelings about you, Prime Minister, and what it is I like about you. So ... um ... here goes."**

He was pleased with his poem, but delivering it was another matter. He coughed a little nervously, clenched his fists to try and stiffen his resolve, opened his mouth to speak – and nothing came out.

He couldn't remember a single word of the poem he had spent the last hour composing.

The first line, he thought to himself, *just remember the first line and the rest will follow.*

He clenched his fists ever more tightly and desperately racked his brain, but nothing came. He looked down at his feet. The small audience shifted uncomfortably in their seats. He was aware of Gloria's intense stare and could feel Honey's anxiety on his behalf as she leant forward, willing him on. Jonny was thinking how brave and thrilling of Harry to stand up and say absolutely nothing; he wished he'd thought of that.

Huxley muttered, **"Rapid breathing, dry mouth, trembling hands – textbook example of performance anxiety."**

Gossie wasn't paying any attention to Harry and only had eyes for Bernie, trying desperately to work out how best to please him.

Harry's fingernails dug into the soft flesh

on his palms. He was starting to feel dizzy.

Just say something! Say anything! Now! NOW!

"When chickens fall out of a tree."

Wait, what?! he thought. Why did I say that! Chickens?? A tree?? Well, I've said it now. Oh, Harry. Need a second line…

"And turnips dress up like a bee."

What am I TALKING ABOUT?!

"We know you as Bernie,

But never as Ernie,

My elbow can count up to three."

I'm going to actually die of embarrassment.

Harry looked around at the blank, confused faces in the audience and thought how his family would probably look equally bewildered and disappointed when he told them he had managed to write a poem but then forget it minutes later.

He pushed desperately on.

"A frog in a hat is not cold.

A cat in a bog is not old.

You're good at your job,

And like corn on the cob,

Your farts are a joy to behold."

Hey, thought Harry, *at least it rhymes.*

"So thank you for leading the nation,

And for providing my education.

You are a man,

My gran likes flan,

I can't think what rhymes with education."

Harry stopped. His audience looked baffled, especially Bernie, who stared at him, breathing heavily through his open mouth. Then Bernie shook his head slowly.

"Thank you," Harry heard himself say

223

and found that he was walking back to his seat. He sat down. There was a smattering of applause. Jonny raised his eyebrows at him in as supportive a manner as he could and Honey gave him a thin smile.

Harry felt sick. The entire future of his family was at stake and surely he'd blown it. If the stakes weren't so high this could have been funny, a story that Maddie and Cy would have enjoyed hearing. But this competition was the only way out of the mess his family was in.

Harry remembered something his mother would tell him. **"Fake it till you make it,"** she'd say. He forced a smile and tried to look like he was pleased with his incredibly weird limericks.

"Right," said Bernie, still clearly confused. **"OK. That was ... um ... who's next?"**

Jonny produced a small table and covered it with a red velvet cloth. He placed a chair behind it and on the table positioned a piece of blank paper, a pen, some scissors and a box of matches.

He took up the pen and began to write.

"Berni Emypm?" said Bernie, squinting. "What's that supposed to say?"

"I think, Prime Minister," said Honey carefully, "that it might be 'Bernie my PM'."

"Yes, I knew that!" said Bernie. "Now quiet please, Miss Plunge."

Honey didn't respond, but Harry thought he detected her face flushing with anger.

Jonny finished writing. Then he picked up the box of matches. He lit a match. Held it near the paper. Then he put the paper in his mouth and ate it. Once he'd swallowed it,

225

he stood up, bowed and returned to his seat. There was silence.

"**WHAT?!**" shouted Bernie after a moment. "**EXCUSE ME BUT WHAT?! What was that supposed to be?**"

Jonny scowled. "**Well ... I like to let my art speak for itself,**" he said. "**Explaining everything would strip it of its power and mystery.**"

"**Power?**" spluttered Bernie. "**That was about as powerful as a butterfly with a chest infection!**"

"**I thought it was interesting,**" said the doctor coldly.

"**Interesting!?**" blurted Bernie.

"**Yes,**" said the doctor. "**Fascinating because I was expecting him to burn the paper or cut it up or both, but he didn't do either. He**

set up an expectation in our minds and then confounded it. Interesting!"

"If that's the sort of thing you find interesting, Doc, good luck to you," said Bernie. "Personally, I'd rather trap my tongue in a door hinge than watch that. And why are you here again? Anyway, who's next? Please let it be something that makes even a tiny bit of sense."

Make sense? thought Jonny bitterly. *What's this obsession with things making sense? The world is complex and mysterious, why can't people relish that rather than trying to flatten everything with logic? Questions are nearly always more interesting than answers.*

Gloria barged past him on her way to the front. "Hey!" he protested half-heartedly.

"Shush, you," she shot back at him. "My

turn. HELLO! So, look, I'm here to talk about our great prime minister."

"This is more like it!" shouted Bernie.

"Our prime minister is strong and I'm strong too," said Gloria, flexing her biceps. "Not just physically, although I think you are all aware of the power I have, but mentally as well. One time I was in a wrestling match against the Breege County champion and we were standing there looking at each other across the mat and she was giving it all 'I'm going to tear you apart' and I was thinking 'no way, I'm going to tear you apart' and we stared at each other and she was waiting for me to speak but I didn't and she was all 'got nothing to say?' and I still didn't say anything and she went 'you scared to speak?' and I still didn't say anything and she was all 'why aren't you saying anything?' and she was all 'say something' but I didn't and she was all 'stop being like that what is wrong with you?' and I could see her confidence crumbling like chalk and sure enough when we started the match I took her down because I'd already won the mental battle. So, yeah, I'm very strong."

Gloria bowed and went to sit down, pausing briefly to point at Bernie and add, **"Like you."** The prime minister did not look pleased.

At least my poems were kind of about Bernie, thought Harry. *That was all about her.*

Next up was Gossie.

"Can I ask our prime minister to join me, please?" she said.

"Not if you're going to make me moo," he responded.

"No!" Gossie laughed a tinkling laugh. **"No**

mooing. Nothing like that. Please, sit."

She motioned to a chair she'd placed facing the audience. Bernie shuffled over to it and sat down.

Gossie, standing just behind Bernie, laid a hand gently on his shoulder. She alone had realized what winning this competition with Bernie in charge was going to take. She alone had worked out what would win it. And it wasn't brains or strength or bravery or artistic sensibility. No, for Bernie the whole world was about one thing only: Bernie. And Gossie was determined to give him exactly what he wanted.

"**We are in the presence of a great man, ladies and gentlemen,**" she began. "**A man who, considering his huge self-sacrifice, bears the heavy burden of public office with dignity. A**

230

man who works his fingers to the bone for us and asks almost nothing in return. A leader. A visionary. A selfless hero. And I don't think any of us appreciate what that involves and how difficult it is to do. I could stand up here and sing a song or make up a poem or a dance or I could eat a piece of paper – sure, I could do all that. But let's face it, there's only one thing that needs to be said and that's this." She lowered her voice. "**From all of us, Prime Minister, 'thank you'.**"

Wow, thought Harry. *That's a bit much, isn't it?*

But then he looked over at Bernie, who was beaming. Gossie, he realized, knew exactly what she was doing.

Harry met Honey Plunge's eye. She nodded ruefully. This was exactly the kind of thing

Farting Bernie had hoped for when he set this challenge. He wanted praise and lots of it and Gossie was clever enough to spot that. Never mind that Gossie probably didn't believe a word of what she was saying, Bernie would love it. *No way to run a competition,* Honey thought to herself. *We'll just end up with the biggest bootlicker winning.*

Huxley was already in position. He had vigorously cleaned his glasses and tightly tied his shoelaces so there was no chance of tripping up on them. He stood upright, legs together, arms straight down by his sides. He had analysed his mistakes from the first round and was confident he could correct them. He would deliver his talk quickly, brightly and efficiently.

"Good day to you, Prime Minister," he

began. "I want to discuss you and your leadership and the thing many people think is your greatest strength – your ability to charm people. The word 'charm' is derived from the word 'charisma': the ability to make other people like you so you can get them to do what you want them to do."

Huh! thought Honey, grumpily. *Bernie's only charming when he wants to be! He's been <u>horrible</u> to me!*

"And my first thought was that charm is a wonderful quality for a leader to have!" said Huxley.

"It is!" agreed Bernie, beaming even harder than he had been. "It is!"

"You are famous for your charm," said Huxley.

"I am!" trilled Bernie.

233

Only by people who've never actually met you, thought Honey bitterly.

"And what could possibly be wrong with being charming?" asked Huxley.

"Nothing!" shouted Bernie. "This is a great speech, young man! Go on!"

"Well, to elucidate, I found four major problems with a leader basing their whole approach on being charming."

"Wait, what? *Problems?*"

"Yes, problems. And here they are. I offer them up in a generous spirit and I hope they will be useful to you going forward."

Bernie narrowed his eyes and said, this time with an icy coldness, "Go on."

Everyone in the room picked up on the threat in Bernie's voice except Huxley, who was focused on being quick, bright and efficient.

"**First**," Huxley said, "if someone is charmed into doing something, they are being led by their emotions, not by logic and reason."

"I see," said Bernie.

"Second, a leader who can charm his people might become addicted to getting that love, sometimes even when it's not appropriate. A good example is your fart machine, sir. People loved it at first, but you keep using it, trying to get a laugh, and it's getting a bit boring now."

"No, it's not! Farts are always funny!" said Bernie, producing an armpit fart. Only Gossie laughed.

"**Third**, charm can hide a person's darker side. A lot of very dangerous people can be charming."

I'm going to kill him, thought Bernie.

"Fourth, charm can make you and those who appreciate your charm feel superior to people who can't see it. You feel better than everyone else."

I _am_ better than everyone else, thought Bernie, *but I've learned not to say it out loud.*

"Is that it?" said Bernie, in a tight voice.

"Yes," said Huxley. "I truly hope this will be useful."

"Oh, it's useful," said Bernie. "Very useful. Guards!"

The guards snapped to attention and all their beavers slid off their heads and under their jaws. They quickly readjusted them.

"Take this boy and place him in a cell in the dungeon. He can remain there until he thinks of four, no, four *hundred* reasons

why I am a great leader and why my charm is a *good* thing."

"Oh, this is fascinating!" said Huxley. "I read a lot about this. When a leader's charm fails to work, they historically turn to force – and that's exactly what you're doing now!"

"Four THOUSAND reasons. Take him away!" barked Bernie, who was so angry he had gone bright red.

"BERNIE!" said Honey, who could take it no longer. "He's a child, Prime Minister!"

"Well then he should act like one!" he said, as the guards led Huxley away.

"I'm sorry, Prime Minister," said Harry, "but this does feel wrong."

Everyone in the room froze. Contradicting the prime minister, they all knew, was a dangerous thing, but Harry carried on regardless.

"Huxley felt he was being helpful. I really believe that. Please don't eliminate him."

Bernie turned and stared cold-eyed at Harry. Jonny felt dizzy with the sudden extra tension in the room. Gossie tried to hide a small smile. Gloria looked a little confused.

Harry had spoken out, but now he was the focus of attention and the room had gone so quiet he wondered whether he was doing the right thing. Was he throwing everything away? But he had to speak.

"If you didn't like what he said, maybe you could just give him last place in this round?" Harry said. "I feel bad for him."

There was silence. Bernie had a bulging

vein on his forehead that looked like it might burst.

"**The thing is, Harry,**" said Honey gently, trying to defuse the situation and protect Harry, "**the prime minister is in charge and what he says goes. I'm sure that if he wanted to eliminate four of you right now and make one the winner without any further rounds he could.**"

Bernie opened his mouth to speak but Honey quickly and firmly continued: "**The king would be interested to hear why the competition had taken a turn like that, but the prime minister, I'm sure, would be able to explain it.**"

Bernie twitched.

"**So, let's keep going and think about the next round, shall we?**" Honey said. "**And well**

done to all of you for making it through."

Everyone looked to Bernie. After what felt like an age he said, "Right, Round Two is over. Gossie wins *by a mile*, Huxley is *eliminated* from the competition and the other three are all second-last. I decide what happens here. Next round is ... um ... I'm hungry so let's see... Next round make me a cake or something nice and the best one wins, but I get to eat them all anyway."

CHAPTER 41

Doctor Face-Problem put her head round the door of King Chisel's bedroom. He was still there in the bed, lying on his back in exactly the same position he had been in the last time she came in.

She listened but could hear nothing. A thought suddenly occurred to her: *I hope he hasn't died! Surely not…*

She concentrated hard. She thought she heard breathing. Perhaps.

I'm sure he's fine, she thought, slowly retreating and gently closing the door.

CHAPTER 42

Honey led Gossie, Gloria, Harry and Jonny down to the palace kitchen so they could prepare for Round Three.

Honey pushed open the big swing doors and walked over to the large table in the middle of the room. Every wall was covered in shelves on which sat pans, pots, dishes, glasses and vast quantities of fresh food.

"Everything you'll need and more will be somewhere in here," said Honey. **"Please help**

yourselves. There are plenty of ovens and cookers. You will be able to make whatever you like. Any questions?"

"Will Huxley be all right?" Harry asked.

"Oh, yes," Honey said. "Don't worry about that. The guys who run the dungeon are good people. They won't let anything bad happen to him."

"Can't believe that he's out of the Crown Duels without warning," said Jonny. "So will someone get booted off every round now?"

"It's very unsettling not knowing what the rules are," said Harry. "Feels like we're trying to play a game without knowing how to play it or even ... what the game really is."

"I'm not a moaner," said Gloria, "but I know what you mean. I don't mind things being tough or difficult; in fact, I quite like that. I like a fight. But I also like to know what I'm trying to do and what will happen if I get it wrong. This contest feels all over the place."

"That's our prime minister," said Honey. "With all respect to him, he does seem to create chaos wherever he goes."

"Well, I think the prime minister is doing an excellent job," said Gossie with a smirk. "Huxley deserved to come last."

"At least he tried to say something interesting and not just suck up to the prime minister like you!" Jonny retorted.

"Jealous!" said Gossie. "Just because I'm in the lead."

"How are you in the lead?!" asked Gloria. "Harry won the first round! You're joint lead."

"That's enough," said Honey. "Come on! No fighting among yourselves! I agree this is a bit of a mess and I'm going to do my best to sort it out. For now, though, you know what you have to do for Round Three: cook something nice. While you do that, I'll talk to the prime minister and see if we can get a scoring system in place that everyone can understand. Make this ... honest and fair. All right?"

The children nodded and Honey went out and shut the door. She took a deep breath. It was time to face the prime minister.

CHAPTER 43

Honey knocked on Bernie's office door.

"WHAT?" came the irritated shout from inside.

"It's Honey, Prime Minister, may I have a word?"

"Now??"

"Please!"

Honey heard a loud sigh from inside.

"Come on then."

She pushed open the door. Bernie was

sitting in front of a mirror.

"Hope I'm not interrupting anything important?" she said.

"You are actually," said Bernie. "I was trying out different ways of combing my hair."

Honey couldn't tell if he was joking or not. He didn't seem to be. And he had a new centre parting which, Honey thought, did *not* suit him.

"What do you want?" he said.

"I was hoping to discuss the Crown Duels. The contestants have questions. And, frankly, so do I."

"Are the questions, *'would you like me to leave you alone, Prime Minister?'* and *'how quickly would you like me to go?'*"

"The children are confused by the scoring system," she said, ignoring him, "and so am I."

"That's deliberate," said the prime minister. "It wouldn't be a test if everyone understood everything. Next question?"

"Couldn't we at least award points for coming first, second and so on? So it's clear who is in the lead?"

"No."

"But..."

"Next question," he said with more than a touch of menace.

Honey persisted. "You threw Huxley in the dungeon. Is this going to be something that happens to contestants?"

"Maybe," said Bernie, turning back to look at himself in the mirror and combing his hair straight back off his forehead. "And maybe not just to the contestants. Bye."

"But Prime Minister—"

"BYE!"

"No, I'm sorry..."

"GUARDS!"

Honey had pushed it as far as she dared. With as much dignity as she could muster, she stood up and left the room.

CHAPTER 44

Harry was struggling with their third task.

Not because he couldn't cook; he could. He was a good cook. In fact, he was extraordinarily good, especially for his age. It was a passion he shared with his mum; they had spent many happy nights together trying out all sorts of different recipes. That was, of course, in better times. Today he had decided to make butternut squash ravioli as a starter – he *loved* ravioli – with a sage and brown butter sauce, and then lemon sole with a grapefruit sabayon and crushed roasted potatoes for the main course. It was all coming together perfectly and looked amazing.

No, Harry was struggling because he knew his family were at home hungry.

With virtually no money, buying food had become increasingly difficult and he knew his mum and dad both skipped meals so that G-Sponge and the children would have enough to eat. Being around vast quantities of food in King Chisel's kitchen and knowing that a load of it would probably end up just being thrown away was tough to take. There was enough food in here to feed half a village; the whole household couldn't possibly get through it all.

He looked over to the other three

contestants.

"Is it worth us coming to an agreement to help each other no matter who wins?" he asked.

"What do you mean?" asked Gloria.

"Well, just that the winner will use their position as king or queen to make sure the other four are not left completely empty-handed."

"Do one!" said Gloria. "Winner takes all. Sounds like you already think you're going to lose."

"No," protested Harry, "but wouldn't it be comforting to know that we'd all win in some little way even if we didn't become the next monarch? Wouldn't that be nice?"

"Nice?" mocked Gloria. "Nice is weak. It's all about winning."

"There's more to life than winning."

"True," said Gloria, "there's also making sure the other person loses. Hahahahaha!"

She kissed her biceps and carried on cooking. Harry looked at Gossie and Jonny, but they were deeply engrossed in what they were doing so he sighed and checked on his roast potatoes.

CHAPTER 45

"I'm going to blend it right now," said Gloria, "so it's as fresh as possible. Then I'll give you both a glass to drink."

"Terrific," said Bernie, but without much enthusiasm. He'd looked at the ingredients Gloria had laid out in front of her, and he didn't much like what he saw.

Standing with him in front of Gloria's workbench, Honey noticed that Bernie had scraped his hair back into a tiny ponytail. She didn't mention it.

Gloria placed steamed chicken breasts, rice, two egg whites, olive oil, spinach and water into her blender. She turned it on for thirty seconds until it was a smooth cold greeny-white paste.

"There it is!" she said proudly. **"The perfect mix of protein and carbs and fat to help your muscles grow."**

She handed the mixture to Bernie. He took the lid off, sniffed and gagged.

"Oh my!" he said, swallowing repeatedly as if trying to get something out of his mouth even though he hadn't drunk any of it. **"That's ... horrific. It smells like ... chicken vomit. I'm not drinking that! You test it."**

He thrust the mixture at Honey.

"Sure," she said. **"I'll give it a go."**

She lifted the thick slop to her mouth, but as she got a whiff of it, she pulled it sharply away again. "**Wow!**" she said, trying to laugh. "**That's ... quite ... something!**"

"**Isn't it?**" said Gloria proudly. "**One thousand calories in there. Saves having to spend ages eating food, which is a right waste of time. Just bosh it.**"

"**I want to bosh it,**" said Honey, wondering what "bosh" meant. "**Here goes!**"

She quickly brought the mixture to her mouth and allowed a dollop to slowly ooze out and flop into her mouth. Instantly regretting it, she swallowed as quickly as she could and tried to keep it down.

"**Oooh,**" she said, tears coming to her eyes. "**It's very chicken-y, isn't it?**"

"**Yes!**" said Gloria. "**Going to bosh it?**"

"I might bosh it in a minute," said Honey. "Need to leave room to bosh some of the other dishes!"

"Gotcha," said Gloria.

"Well done, Gloria," said Honey. "Thank you."

"Disgusting," said Bernie loudly, moving on to Jonny's table. "Absolutely disgusting."

Gloria flushed. She was a tough girl, but this last comment made her feel unexpectedly tearful. She couldn't understand why the prime minister wouldn't even *try* her drink. How could he judge food just by looking at it? It wasn't fair. She understood when one person beat someone else by running faster or lifting more or throwing further, but this ... she did not understand this. She looked around at the others, embarrassed to be feeling this way.

Harry gave her a smile of encouragement and Gloria, despite herself, smiled back.

Jonny was sitting in a chair in front of a small square table. He was wrapped entirely in cling film, from head to toe, with holes cut out for his face and hands. As Bernie and Honey came over, he picked up a pair of scissors and began to painstakingly cut through the cling film that covered the table, peeling it back to reveal knives, forks, glasses and plates – also wrapped entirely in cling film.

Bernie and Honey watched in bewilderment.

"What's going on?" asked Bernie. Jonny said nothing but continued to slice through cling film. It took several minutes but eventually he had freed a fork, a glass of water and a plate. On the plate were about thirty French fries, all individually wrapped in cling film. He began to cut them free with the scissors.

"What in the name of all things holy is going on?!" demanded Bernie.

Jonny said nothing but continued slicing through the cling film, one chip at a time.

"Maybe it's a statement about how we have too much packaging on food?" suggested Honey. **"About waste, possibly?"**

"I'll tell you what it's a waste of," said

Bernie, walking off. **"My time!"**

Honey reached over and took a chip, wondering whether she was supposed to touch the art, let alone eat it. It was soggy.

"Well done, Jonny!" she said brightly, and joined Bernie at Harry's table. Jonny gulped and managed to nod his thanks.

Harry had placed a crisp white tablecloth over his table, on which white napkins, cutlery, glasses, a jug of fresh water and his attractive-looking dishes were neatly arranged. There was a vase containing a couple of small red flowers and two chairs. He offered one to Honey, who smiled at him and sat down.

"I'll get my own chair then, shall I?" said Bernie huffily, plonking himself down.

"What do we have here, Harry?" asked Honey.

"Well," Harry said, pointing to one of the dishes, "I've done a butternut squash ravioli as a starter..."

"Butternut squash?!" said Bernie with distaste.

"Yes," said Harry. "Do you like butternut squash?"

"I've never had it," said Bernie. "I like meat with my pasta."

"Meat is nice, sure, but wait until you try my ravioli..."

"I don't like trying new things," said Bernie, folding his arms and looking grumpy.

Honey had speared a square of ravioli and popped it into her mouth.

"Oh, that's delicious, Harry, well done," she said. "Give it a try, Prime Minister!"

"I. Don't. Like. New. Things." Bernie pouted.

"What else have you got?"

"The main course is lemon sole..."

"FISH?!" shrieked Bernie. "FISH?! I hate fish! Yuck! Eating fish is like licking the bottom of a boat!"

"Is it?" said a surprised Harry.

"Yes, it's like having a walrus sneeze in your face."

"Really?"

"Fish weird me out with their eyes and bones and slimy bodies. What's wrong with all of you? Why can't one of you just cook me a nice meal?"

"I made it with crushed roast potatoes," said Harry, hoping to find something in what he had made that would appeal to Bernie.

"And now they'll taste of fish too!" said Bernie. "Why didn't you make me something

I like?"

"Oh," said Harry. "I don't know what you like."

"And you haven't taken the time to find out, have you? Disappointed in you, young man. I had high hopes for you."

Before Harry could answer, Bernie jumped up and crossed the room to Gossie's table, high-fiving her enthusiastically.

Honey smiled apologetically. "I'd better go with him," she said. "The ravioli was magnificent, Harry."

Harry smiled back as best he could. His head was spinning. How could he possibly have known what the prime minister liked to eat? It seemed like this competition was all about Bernie rather than finding out what the contestants were capable of. Once again, he had the inescapable thought that he'd blown it. He looked at his food and thought, *that's a really good meal.*

Gossie had baked a cake. She had covered it, sloppily, with bright pink frosting and piped something in red icing across the top. Bernie tried to work out what it said.

"Does that say, 'Bummie in Bust'?" he asked her.

She laughed a tinkly, ingratiating laugh. **"You're so funny, Prime Minister!"** she said. **"You always make me laugh. It says, 'Bernie is Best'. Unfortunately, I dropped the cake while bringing it in from the garden. I was icing it out there because"** – here she dropped her voice – **"I don't entirely trust the others not to steal my ideas."** She raised her eyebrows in a knowing way. **"Anyway. Not my fault. The**

267

goat got in my way."

"Rodney Dangertubes?"

"Yes, it bleated and I dropped the cake in fright."

"You poor thing. Can I try some of this cake then?"

"I wouldn't."

"Why not?"

"It fell into some of Rodney Dangertubes' droppings. I tried to clean it up as best as possible, but there may still be some of his doings in the cake."

"I see. So those are not raisins?"

"No."

"Well, 'Bernie is Best' is nice."

"Thank you."

"You win this round!"

"Oh, thank you, Prime Minister!"

Honey was appalled. "Really, Prime Minister? Her cake has poo in it!"

"She won for style," hissed Bernie. "Leave it."

"Style? You couldn't even read the message!" said Honey.

"I'm warning you, Miss Lounge..."

"Plunge."

"Whatever."

"Her cake has ACTUAL POO in it! How can it win?!"

"Right, that's it!" barked Bernie. "Gossie wins, second is ... um ... wow, they were all terrible. Second is plastic boy. Third is Gloria and Harry is last because *fish*."

"In that case, Prime Minister, I can no longer be a part of this."

"I would be quiet if I were you, Miss Munch,

before I make you eat some of the winning cake!"

"It's Miss Plunge," she said, full of righteous indignation. "And you may do your worst because the way you are running this competition is a total disgrace and I will not stand quietly by any longer. I have done my best to see things from every side and to attempt to bring calm and harmony, but there comes a point, Prime Minister, when enough is enough. You are running the Crown Duels as a popularity contest. You are showing no respect to our king. You are showing no respect to our country. Your behaviour is quite appalling, and I won't hold my tongue for a moment longer. I quit. I will stay only to make sure the children are not treated—"

"YOU DO NOT QUIT, MISS CRUNGE, I AM

FIRING YOU!" Bernie screamed, incandescent with rage. **"I DID IT! NOT YOU! ME! YOU ARE FIRED! I HATE YOU SO MUCH! GET OUT! GET OUT! GUARDS! GUARDS!**"

Honey, holding back tears, walked to the kitchen door, pulled it open and was startled to find King Chisel standing behind it in his pyjamas. The king groaned, swayed and fell forward, hitting the ground with a thump.

CHAPTER 46

The king opened his eyes and tried to focus. Was that ... a fuzzy ... upside down ... *beaver*? Was he dreaming again? He was aware of people in the room, whispering, the rustling of clothes, someone gently snoring.

"He's awake!" called a voice. "I saw his eyes flutter. Out of the way, guard."

The fuzzy beaver withdrew and a figure leant in.

"Can you hear me, Your Royal Highness?"

King Chisel attempted to open his mouth to respond but couldn't.

"Take your time. It appears you sleepwalked down into the kitchen and fell over. The prime minister has been running things while you have been asleep."

And suddenly the blurry figures came into sharp focus, his hearing snapped into place and it felt like his mind had kick-started. Standing around the bed were the doctor, Farting Bernie and Honey. Two guards stood by the door.

"An extraordinarily vivid experience, followed by total nothingness," King Chisel said quietly. **"Most peculiar. Like a bird flapping through the void, the dark, then suddenly emerging into colour and mayhem and sensation, almost overwhelming, then**

back to the dark and the void once again."

"Such is life," said the doctor.

"The Crown Duels?" the king said. His mouth felt dry.

"Ah, yes!" piped up Bernie. "Coming along nicely, sir."

"What stage are you at?"

"One contestant has been eliminated."

"Eliminated? Why?"

"Well ... um ... he was ... too clever," said the prime minister.

"Too clever?"

"Yes." Bernie nodded. "Would have been useless as king. No offence."

King Chisel turned to Honey. "Do you agree that the contestant was too clever? That he should have been eliminated?" he asked her.

She looked to Bernie, who narrowed his eyes.

"Tell me the truth," said King Chisel. "Never mind him."

"Huxley is clever, but I thought his elimination was unfair," said Honey, lifting her chin.

"He ... criticized me," said Bernie. "I can take a joke, but he should have respected the fact that I am the prime minister and he shouldn't say anything bad about me, ever."

"Nonsense," said King Chisel. "Your ego can't take even the slightest criticism. Huxley will be brought back into the contest."

"But..."

"No buts! Do it!"

"Yes, Your Highness."

"Any other news?"

Honey raised her hand.

"Yes, Honey."

"Rodney Dangertubes has escaped, sire. Seems he upset one of the contestants by bleating at the wrong moment. Whoever it was hacked the rope and let him wander off. No one can find him."

"That goat is a nuisance."

"Yes, sire."

"But that gives me an idea. Get the contestants together."

"But Your Majesty!" said Bernie. "I have several more rounds already prepared for them. Next, I was going to get them each to make a statue of me and then I wanted them to design and build their own fireworks which would spell my name when they exploded and then I was going to get them to decorate my house and then..."

"STOP!" said the king. "You are shameless.

We will be doing none of those things, Prime Minister." He took a deep breath. "I had a whole range of tests and trials lined up, but I think I will give them one last winner-takes-all challenge instead. Something difficult that will take intelligence and courage and the ability to charm a grumpy goat. My recent ill health has made it clear to me that we need to get this sorted out as soon as possible. So this is my plan.

"Rodney Dangertubes is loose somewhere out there. He can't get out of the palace grounds, but the palace grounds are *big*. Knowing Rodney as I do, he will be thrilled to have gained his freedom and won't want to be found. Tell the contestants this: whoever finds and returns Rodney to the palace shall be king or queen. As simple as that.

"First, though, they will need to find a way *out* of this palace. They will begin in the dungeons. I will have a think, come up with a plan and issue some instructions. Sometimes, Smitherington-Piffle, a little planning can be a useful thing."

Bernie snorted. He hated being lectured like this. It made him feel like he was a seven-year-old schoolboy again, unhappy and homesick, back at the awful boarding school he went to when he was little because his parents had wanted him out of the way.

"Also, you know, and I know," continued the king, "that many dangers lie in wait for unsuspecting souls outside these palace walls. More dangerous than a grumpy goat, that's certain. Let's see what they are made of. And remind them: they are not to help each other.

I want no clubbing together. That would only confuse the issue and I hate confusion. They have to do it alone otherwise they will be disqualified. Now go. I need to rest."

The guards saluted and the doctor, Honey Plunge and the prime minister began to file out of the room.

"And, Prime Minister," said King Chisel, "you are to be extremely nice and kind to Honey Plunge. Do you understand?"

"I suppose," said Bernie, moodily.

"And, Prime Minister, let's release Fortuna Piranha into the grounds too."

"Really?!" said Bernie, shocked. "Another goat? That's going to make things extremely confusing for the contestants."

"Exactly. Let's see how smart they are. Let's see if they can tell a male goat from a female goat."

"But what if Rodney Dangertubes finds Fortuna Piranha first? Things could get a little spicy!"

"Let them get spicy," said the king. "No one said this would be easy."

FORTUNA PIRANHA

CHAPTER 47

Five cells; five children.

The cells were all empty, not a chair, table or window. Huxley had been pleased to see them all trooping down to join him in the dungeons and even more delighted to be told that he had been allowed back into the Crown Duels – he'd been worrying about how disappointed his mum would be. However, that joy turned quickly to confusion as the other four contestants were locked in cells on either side of him.

"Welcome!" he said. "What are you doing here? Did you all do something wrong?"

"Can't tell you," said Harry, not unkindly. "We've been told over and over that we can't help each other in even the smallest way and will be disqualified if we do."

Honey arrived and faced them through the bars.

"First, I want to apologize for how the competition has gone so far. You all deserve better. This was not what the king intended, but he's back in charge now. This is not only the *final* round but the *only round that matters.*"

Gossie drew in her breath sharply at this; things had been going well for her, so these latest developments were desperately annoying. In contrast, the others looked hopeful; maybe order was about to be restored.

Honey went on. "**Your challenge is this. You have to escape the cells you are in, find a way out of the palace and track down the king's goat, Rodney Dangertubes, who is missing. Bring the goat back to the palace and you will be the next king or queen.**"

"That's it?" asked Gloria. "**Find a goat?**"

"Um ... yes," said Honey.

"So, let me get this straight," said Huxley. "The new monarch in this country is being decided by a goat treasure hunt?"

"That is correct, Huxley," said Honey. "I can give you the following information about Rodney. He's a goat, he's hungry and he's grumpy. And, of course, he's a boy goat – not a girl. That's important. Are you all ready? Go!"

All five of them ran to the front of their cages.

Gloria grabbed two of the iron bars and, with every ounce of strength she possessed in her body, tried to prise them apart.

Huxley inspected his cage closely, looking for structural weak points or a clue of some sort.

Jonny sat down and closed his eyes, trying to imagine what he would do if he were the king organizing a challenge like this. Then he began to channel the king from the little he'd seen of him. He became lost in the king's character…

Harry dropped to his hands and knees and began to carefully feel his way across the floor. He wondered whether there was a secret hatch or panel in the ground that could be lifted to uncover an escape tunnel of some kind.

Gloria was sweating profusely, but the iron bars had budged not even the tiniest bit.

Huxley was still examining the first bar in minute detail.

Jonny was having a great time pretending to be the king.

Harry had finished feeling his way round the floor and discovered nothing. He turned his attention to the ceiling.

Gossie looked at them all. Then she went to the bars and called, **"Guard! Can you come**

285

over here?"

The guard came over to Gossie. She leant forward and whispered something into his ear. The guard listened, nodded, took out a key, slid it into the lock and opened Gossie's door. She walked out, waved to the others, then ran off.

"WHAT?!" shouted Gloria. "YOU LET HER OUT??? LET ME OUT!"

The guard shook his head and returned to his position. Everyone else began pleading with him.

"Let me out!" called Jonny.

"Over here! Over here!" shouted Harry.

"You let her out!" pleaded Huxley. "Let me out too!"

"LET ME OUT OR I'LL TEAR YOU APART!" shouted Gloria.

"Come on, sir," said Jonny. "I know what

it feels like to do something you don't necessarily agree with. I understand you. Let me out, please."

This last plea, for some reason, worked wonders on the guard, who strode over to Jonny's cell, unlocked the door and let him out. Jonny bolted for the exit.

"**WHAT!?!?**" bellowed Gloria. "**YOU LET OUT THAT NUMPTY AND YOU WON'T OPEN THE DOOR FOR ME?!**" She grabbed the iron bars and began to wrench them backwards and forwards. Her eyes bulged out of their sockets. The bars still didn't budge.

Huxley sat with his eyes closed for a moment, thinking hard. "**Got it!**" he exclaimed, and beckoned the guard over. He whispered in the guard's ear. The guard unlocked Huxley's cell and he scampered off.

Gloria stopped trying to wrench the bars apart and stood panting. **"Hang on!"** she exclaimed. **"I think I've worked it out. OK, come here, guard."**

The guard did as asked, Gloria leant forward and … licked his ear. He yelped.

"What are you doing!" shrieked the guard.

"I thought that's what the others did!" she protested.

"No!" said the guard, rubbing his ear vigorously with the sleeve of his jacket. **"Gross!"**

"Sorry," said Gloria. **"Oh, please let me out!"**

"Sure," said the guard, and unlocked the door. Gloria roared in triumph and bolted off as fast as she could, leaving Harry the only one still locked in.

"Well, don't I feel daft?" said Harry to the guard. **"I have no idea how to get out."**

CHAPTER 48

When Jonny had nearly reached the end of the winding corridor, he heard running water. Turning a corner, he saw where it was coming from. In front of him a wall of water was cascading down in front of a brick wall with tremendous force.

There was no sign of Gossie.

Jonny was not a strong swimmer. Even putting his head underwater made him feel claustrophobic and anxious. But there seemed to be no other way through. He edged towards the waterfall and saw that attached to the wall the water was cascading down was a metal ladder leading up.

This appeared to be the only way out.

Jonny decided the only way he was going to get through this was to pretend he was Gloria. She'd surely love a challenge like this. He closed his eyes and imagined he was strong and muscled and in possession of a super-competitive personality. He clenched his fists, slapped himself hard on the shoulder and screamed, **"PURPLE BUNIONS, GRILLED ONIONS!"**, ran to the ladder and began to climb.

The force of the water bearing down on him was extraordinary. He could barely cling on, but he climbed slowly, roaring and shouting in his best imitation of Gloria.

He felt the ladder shudder and looked down. There below him was the real Gloria climbing the ladder with great intensity.

"PUNCH MY LUNCH!" she shouted.

"FLIP IT, YOU LONG JELLY!" shouted Jonny in response, feeling another surge of power as he did so. He *was* Gloria in that moment, and it helped him to make good progress up the ladder.

Behind them, Huxley, who had been overtaken in the tunnel by Gloria, had made it to the bottom of the ladder and he too began to climb. He got three steps up when the battering he took from the falling water made him lose his grip and he fell to the ground.

In his cell, Harry was becoming desperate.

"They'll have found Rodney Dangertubes by now!" he said to the guard. "Why won't you let me out?"

The guard shrugged.

"Did the others give you money? Or make a special signal? Or say a magic word?"

There was a little twitch of the guard's eyebrows at that last question.

"A magic word? Is there a magic word?" Harry remembered one of G-Sponge's favourite sayings: *What's the magic word?* "Please?" he ventured.

"That's it," said the guard brightly. "Thought you'd never get it. Good luck."

He opened the door and Harry ran off, feeling just a bit put out that Gossie and Gloria had got out before him in a test of politeness.

"**Thank you!**" said Harry, politely, as he ran off.

CHAPTER 49

Huxley had made eight attempts to climb the ladder and every time he'd been washed off before reaching the fifth rung. He sat on the cold hard ground, sopping wet.

Think, Huxley, he urged himself. *Doing the same thing over and over and over again and expecting a different result is not smart. Be smart.*

He examined the brick walls along the corridor and on either side of the waterfall. It

294

was dark, only a little light spilled down from the opening above, but slowly his eyes were adjusting.

Bricks, bricks and more bricks.

Only…

One of them had a small perfectly round hole in it. *Odd.*

Huxley tentatively pushed a finger into the

hole. There was a click, just audible over the roar of the water, and the end of the brick popped out. Huxley placed his fingers around the end of it and pulled. It swung open like a small door. Behind it was a tap. Huxley turned the tap and the water stopped falling.

That's better, he thought.

Harry came tearing round the corner, saw a soaking Huxley and the ladder, and screeched to a halt.

"You OK, Huxley?"

"You can't help me! And I don't need help."

"You need a towel!"

"Very funny. Go!"

"Good luck!"

Harry leapt on to the bottom rung and was up it like a shot.

CHAPTER 50

Harry raced out into the palace grounds, scanning the horizon for any signs of an escaped goat. He could hear Gloria hacking her way through some bushes in the distance, shouting at the top of her voice, **"GOAT! GOAT! COME HERE OR YOU'LL REGRET IT!"**

Wait, thought Harry, slowing down. *Let's think this through for a second.*

The goat could be *anywhere.* The palace grounds were vast. Gardens, ponds, the bottom fountains and the orchards, plus the wild meadows, a river and the enormous vegetable garden. Where might a goat go? Maybe the goat was hungry. He had bleated when he saw Gossie's cake. The vegetable garden seemed an obvious place to start. But surely the vegetable garden would be well-protected.

Harry thought some more. Perhaps he should treat this as if he were a proper detective? How would a detective begin to find a missing person/goat?

He needed a lead. A clue. A starting point for his search. He needed information. Where to find it? Where to begin?

OK, think, Harry. What do we know about the goat? We know its name – Rodney Dangertubes. We know … it can be grumpy.

We know it bleats. And poos, because Gossie got goat droppings on her cake. We know … it was last seen by Gossie when she was trying to decorate her cake. Coming back from the garden to the kitchen, she'd said…

Harry decided to start there. He began to run in the direction of the kitchen, which he remembered from earlier. He ran past an open window on the north side of the palace and inside he saw Huxley sitting at a desk.

Harry stopped and peeped in. Huxley was writing furiously, head bent over a piece of paper. Harry craned closer. Were those maths equations?

"Psst," said Harry.

"I can't help you!" said Huxley without looking up.

"I don't want you to help me. I don't have

a clue what you're doing. But why aren't you out looking for Rodney?"

"I'm working out the mathematical probability of where Rodney might have gone, to help narrow down my search. I'm trying to use mathematics, logic and the latest behavioural goat research to predict his movements." Huxley sighed. "Trouble is there are so many variables it's going to take a while."

"Oh, right," said Harry, in awe of Huxley's braininess. "Good luck!"

"You too," said Huxley, not looking up from his calculations.

Harry rounded the corner of the palace and ran across the croquet lawn to the kitchen door. There he found the mess of icing and goat droppings, confirming Gossie's story. He looked around for any other clues.

From this spot, Rodney could have gone off in three main directions. Left to the bottom fountains, straight to the vegetable gardens or right towards the king's orchard.

He looked for any signs of hoofprints, but it was a lovely summer's day and the ground was hard and undisturbed.

A rose bush a little way off to the right caught his eye. Something seemed to be snagged on it. A scrap of … what was that? He walked over and his heart soared. A chunk of what looked like goat hair clung to a thorn. Had Rodney Dangertubes brushed up against this rose bush while passing this way? Walking from the kitchen to the orchard? It was Harry's best and, frankly, *only* lead, so he decided to go with it.

He took off towards the king's orchard.

Running along the path, he kept an eye out for any other clues but spotted nothing. He'd heard of trackers who could place their ear to the ground and detect sounds that would direct them to their prey, but he thought he'd feel pretty daft lying on the ground with his ear to the grass. The one thing he could hear was Gloria, somewhere to his left, shouting, **"I'M WARNING YOU, GOAT! DON'T HIDE FROM ME! WHERE ARE YOU?!"**

Harry reached the orchard. It was huge, stretching as far as he could see in all directions, a huge and glorious assortment of beautiful trees, all groaning under the weight of apples and pears. He searched for clues or tracks, even sniffing the air in case he could pick up some sort of scent.

Who am I kidding? he thought. *I'm not a dog! What a shame Lemon isn't here.*

Dodging in and out of trees, he cast around desperately but found nothing and saw no one. Suddenly he came to a high stone wall – no goat was getting over that. A dead end.

He turned around and ran back the way he came.

It turns out that one tree looks pretty much the same as another, and it wasn't long before Harry began to wonder if he was lost. He ran frantically, ducking and diving, took a right turn, then a left. Stopped, turned, ran back. He was considering climbing one of the trees to try and get his bearings when he heard voices. He stopped to listen. Two voices whispering urgently. He crept towards them as quietly as he could. A loud, irritating voice and a soft, gentle one. Bernie and Gossie! What were they doing? Harry crept closer, trying to hear over the pounding in his ears from all that running.

"You are a true leader," Gossie was saying. "Every sensible person in the country thinks so."

"Well, I'm... That's terrific," replied Bernie.

"The greatest leader we have ever had," Gossie continued. "It would be an honour to be your monarch."

She's flattering him again, thought Harry. *And he absolutely loves it.*

304

He peered around a tree trunk. Bernie was indeed glowing.

"**You seem like a very intelligent young woman,**" he said. "**I think you'd make an excellent monarch, have done from the start. Let's try and make it happen.**"

The prime minister was offering to help Gossie win the Crown Duels! Despite having seen how Bernie had responded to Gossie's flattery that day, it was still a shock. Harry gasped in surprise.

"**What was that?**" asked Gossie. "**Did you hear something?**"

"**I don't think so,**" said Bernie.

"**OK,**" said Gossie. "**Anyway, thanks for the tip-off about how to get out of the cells.**"

"**My pleasure. Right. Here's the plan. I've found Rodney – he is in the meadow. Follow**

this wall down until it ends, then turn left. You can't miss him. The king asked me to release Fortuna Piranha as a decoy, but I tied her up to a tree out of the way. So take the goat in the meadow not the goat tied to the tree. Got it?"

"Got it! You are so clever!"

"I sure am, future queen!" said Bernie. "Now, remind me what we agreed?"

"That you can be prime minister for ever and ever."

Again, Harry gasped, but Bernie was clapping and neither turned round.

"What if something goes wrong? If someone gets to the goat before me?" asked Gossie.

"We'll say they helped each other, get them disqualified. I've thought of everything. Now, go! I'll see you back at the palace."

Gossie turned and ran alongside the wall in the direction Bernie had indicated. Bernie strutted off in what Harry realized must be the way back to the palace.

Harry waited till he'd gone. Then he leapt over the wall and ran as fast as he could along the other side of it, hoping Gossie couldn't hear him.

CHAPTER 51

Gloria tore through another bush.

"GOAT!?" she shouted. Her frustration was building. *Show me a weight and I'll lift it*, she thought. *Give me an opponent and I'll fight them. Show me a mountain and I'll climb it. But this is just annoying.*

Bursting into a clearing, she spotted a peculiar sight – a large hairy bundle inching across the grass. What was *that*? Was that a goat? Gloria was a city girl and she had never seen a goat up close.

Slowly and cautiously, Gloria approached it. The creature was moving erratically, sometimes a couple of paces at once, sometimes pausing. It looked to Gloria like a rug that had come to life, but maybe that's just what goats looked like when they were … eating? Resting? She had no idea.

What in the world was it? She called out. **"Hello?"**

The pile stopped moving. There seemed to be no head, no tail. No front or back.

"Hello?" she tried again, and this time got a response.

"Go away, Gloria," it whispered.

"Jonny?"

"Yes."

"What are you doing?"

"I am channelling goat. I have become goat. I am essence of goat. I am hoping Rodney will recognize a kindred spirit and come to me."

"I see," said Gloria. "Has it ever occurred to you that you're a bit strange?"

The hairy pile sagged a little, Gloria heard a long sigh and then Jonny threw off the rug he was hiding under.

"Really?" he said wearily. "Gloria, you lift heavy things up and then put them down again in the same place. Over and over again. All day. And you think I'm strange?"

CHAPTER 52

As he ran, Harry came to a goat tied to a tree. He had an idea.

This was Fortuna Piranha: the "wrong" goat. Quickly, Harry untied Fortuna and, holding her lead tightly in his hand, carried on running. Fortuna seemed like a mild-mannered goat and was quite happy lolloping along next to Harry.

They came to the end of the wall and Harry slowed. He was on the right-hand side of the wall. On the left-hand side was Gossie. He peeked round the wall and, sure enough, there she was. She was in the meadow, heading towards a creature in the distance – Rodney Dangertubes.

Harry had to act quickly.

He headed directly towards Gossie. As he got closer, he could see she had slowed down and was approaching Rodney nervously. The male goat did seem like a mean customer. Harry saw a big dead branch lying on the ground in front of him and deliberately jumped on to it. It broke with a loud snap. Gossie whipped round.

"Harry!" said Gossie, all smiles.

"Oh, hi, Gossie," Harry said casually, and carried on walking.

"Wait a second," said Gossie.

"Can't help you, Gossie, you know that."

Then he stopped. "Look, Gossie – I know I shouldn't, but the truth is I don't want you getting hurt. That goat you're next to – I untied it from a tree over there a few minutes ago thinking it was Rodney Dangertubes. And then wished I hadn't because she's a vicious thing."

Gossie blinked. "She?"

"That's right. That's a girl goat. Anyway, please don't get hurt by her. Be careful." And Harry made to go.

"Wait!" called Gossie. "How can you tell it's a 'she'? They both look the same to me."

Harry shook his head. "That's all I can say." And he walked on, hoping Gossie had taken the bait.

Almost immediately there was a thundering of goat hooves and Rodney came running over. Rodney skidded to a halt in front of Harry.

Clearly, Rodney had sensed Fortuna on the other side of the wall.

Rodney stood square on to Harry with his head held high, tilted slightly forward. His back was arched and his hackles were raised. Harry could feel the aggression pouring out of him and it was frightening. Harry held up his hands.

"Whoa, boy!" he said, his voice shaking with fear. **"Whoa. Good boy."**

"Good boy?" said Gossie, marching back over. **"I thought you said that was a female goat?"**

"Got confused," explained Harry, **"because she's scaring me!"**

He held up his hands and made some

314

soothing sounds, but this did not have the desired effect. Behind him, Fortuna peered around the wall. Rodney reared up on his back legs and slammed the front ones down hard into the ground, causing Harry to jump and Fortuna Piranha to bleat frantically. It occurred to Harry that he was standing in between Rodney and Fortuna. Perhaps he ought to get out of the way? Harry was never one to pick a fight when a fight wasn't necessary, and he wasn't about to start now, especially with such a strong and grumpy goat.

"Why don't I leave you two alone for a second, ma'am?" he said. **"You can have a little chat."**

He edged away and stood beside Gossie, who was watching with narrowed eyes. Fortuna was bleating and so was Rodney.

Between them they made quite a racket. Then Fortuna lowered her rear end to the ground and peed.

"**When you gotta go, you gotta go!**" joked Harry.

"**Hmm,**" said Gossie.

Just then, over the bleating of the goats, there was another noise. Harry and Gossie turned to see that a screaming Gloria, arms in the air, was running right at them. She skidded to a halt. "**Stand back!**" she yelled. No one moved. Rodney and Fortuna eyed her warily. "**Two goats?**" she said. "**Which one's Rodney Dangertubes? NO! Don't tell me! You mustn't help me! Don't tell me! Don't help me!**"

"**Thank goodness you're here!**" said Gossie. "**Harry was almost attacked. You've arrived just in time to help. I'll get this other goat**

316

– which is definitely not Rodney – out of the way so you two can calm Rodney down."

Gossie grabbed Fortuna and sauntered off, clearly under the impression she had Rodney and was going to win. Which should have been good news for Harry – only now, Gloria was on the scene, confusing matters.

"So this is Rodney," said Gloria, pointing at the real Rodney, the goat left behind. "But then why isn't Gossie taking him – oh, never mind." She grabbed his collar. "Come on, buster."

Harry wasn't sure how to handle this. He'd never be able to just grab Rodney from Gloria. Also, Rodney had decided he simply wasn't going anywhere. Annoyed at losing his friend, he dug his hooves in.

"Stupid goat!" Gloria complained. "Move!" She pulled him with all her might, but Rodney

Dangertubes stayed put. Gloria bent down and went eyeball to eyeball with him. **"No, you listen to me, goat. We can do this my way, or we can do it the wrong way. Which is it going to be?"**

Rodney lowered his chin threateningly.

"Oh, that's the way you want it?" said Gloria. **"You're on, Goatface!"**

And she lowered her chin too, placing her forehead against Rodney's, and she began to push.

She's not really going head-to-head with a goat, is she? thought Harry.

Rodney braced and pushed back, lowering his body and driving forward with his legs. Gloria did the same, grunting with the effort. **"I'm never going to give up, Goatface, you hear me? Never!"**

Goat and girl strained every sinew. Rodney was now silent, all his concentration and all his strength focused on Gloria. Incredibly, Gloria held her own, neither moving forward or back. Her strength was impressive. It was a matter of which one of them could keep this effort up the longest.

They were both shaking with the effort. Then, out of nowhere, Fortuna Piranha reappeared, running at Gloria from the side and knocking her clean off her feet. Where had she come from?

"Are you all right?" Harry asked Gloria, as she lay face down, breathing heavily. "Here, let me help you up."

"Well, well, well," said a voice. Harry and Gloria looked up to see Bernie and Gossie standing there, arms crossed, two guards behind them.

"Did you hear that, Gossie?" asked Bernie. "Harry just helped Gloria. And earlier you saw Gloria helping him."

"Did I?" asked Gossie, and then realized that Bernie was encouraging her to lie. "Oh yes! I did. I saw Gloria helping Harry. Looks like they are both disqualified!"

"It's all over for you two," snarled Bernie. "Over. Disqualified. Dungeons. Guards, seize them!"

CHAPTER 53

A door in the palace opened and Huxley Beeline came tearing out, shouting, **"I've got it! I did the calculations! I've worked out the most likely place to find Rodney!"**

He tore across the palace lawn, passing *as he did* a bundle of rugs. Jonny stuck his head out from underneath and watched Huxley disappear into the distance.

This isn't working, thought Jonny. *Embodying the goat is not summoning the*

goat. I need to try another tack.

He threw off the rug and ran as fast as he could in the direction Huxley Beeline had made a beeline for.

CHAPTER 54

"Seize them, guards!" cried Bernie. "They collaborated and must be disqualified."

The guards lurched towards Harry and Gloria and as they did so their beavers slid off their heads and under their chins. They stopped to readjust them.

"Get on with it!" cried Bernie.

"Our beavers!" shouted a guard.

"Never mind the stupid beavers, grab them!" the prime minister bellowed.

The guards were appalled. "**Our first duty, sir, is to our beavers. You surely know that?**"

Meanwhile, Rodney and Fortuna began wandering off.

"**The goats!**" said Gossie. "**They're going to get away.**"

"**We'll deal with the goats once these ruffians are arrested,**" said Bernie.

"**Ruffians?**" said Gloria, who had got her breath back and was furious. "**How dare you!**"

"**ARREST THEM!!**" screamed Bernie. The guards lunged at Gloria and Harry, but once again suffered a beaver malfunction. The guards dutifully stopped to readjust.

"**This is the weirdest chase in history!**" remarked Harry. "**We haven't moved an inch and they still haven't caught us!**"

Gloria laughed, despite herself. "**Too right.**"

"What's going on here?" yelled a surprised Huxley, arriving breathlessly. "My calculations told me I'd find Rodney here and – oh, there he is!"

Not far behind him came Jonny, no longer wearing his rugs.

"What?!" was all Jonny could manage when he took in the scene.

Bernie spluttered with rage. "What are you two doing here! This isn't the plan! Go away!"

"Why?" asked Huxley. "There's Rodney! Standing next to what is clearly a female goat, if I have my caprine biology straight. The crown will be mine!"

"Caprine?" asked Gossie.

"Yes, it means 'pertaining to goats' from the Latin caprinus meaning goat," said Bernie. "BUT THAT'S NOT IMPORTANT RIGHT NOW!

This is getting out of control! You" — he pointed at Huxley and Jonny — "are not meant to be here. And you" — he pointed at Harry and Gloria — "are meant to be in a dungeon."

Huxley ignored him and made for Rodney. So did Jonny. The guards turned their heads to see what was happening and their beavers fell off. They began to readjust them. Again.

"THAT'S IT!!" shrieked Bernie, who had gone a very peculiar shade of red. "THAT'S IT! ENOUGH OF THESE GAMES! I'M TAKING OVER. THAT'S IT!" He reached into his jacket and pulled out a gun.

Gloria gasped, Jonny gasped, Harry gasped, Huxley gasped and both the guards gasped. Everyone except Gossie gasped.

"MOVE OVER THERE!" Bernie shouted. "ALL OF YOU. MOVE OVER THERE. OR I'LL

SHOOT! Gossie, stand with me."

They all obeyed. Even the guards shuffled over, with their helmets swinging under their chins.

"Gossie, collect Rodney Dangertubes and take him to the palace. I'll deal with this lot."

"Right," said Gossie. "Which one's the boy goat?"

"The moody one. Use Fortuna Piranha as bait."

"Right."

She jogged over to Fortuna, grabbed her by the collar and yanked her back towards the group. This upset Fortuna, who shook off Gossie and took off like a rocket, racing round and round the trunk of the huge oak tree they were all standing under, before leaping up into its branches.

"What's going on?" asked Bernie, not taking his eyes off the others.

"Fortuna is in the tree," Gossie said.

"What?"

"She ran up into the tree. I didn't know goats could climb trees."

"OF COURSE THEY CAN CLIMB TREES!!" Bernie bellowed. "They are amazing climbers. Have you never heard of mountain goats? They can climb massive mountains!"

Rodney, seeing his sweetheart up in the tree, decided to join her. In a flash he was standing on the branch next to her.

"So the good news," said Gossie, "is that Rodney will indeed follow Fortuna anywhere, so we know that works. The bad news is that they're both now up the tree."

"WHAT?!!!" Bernie was bright purple.

"What are you going to do now, Bernie?" asked Harry.

"You shush," said Bernie.

"Fart?" said Gloria, and they all giggled.

"I said quiet!"

"Or what?" said Jonny.

"I bet that gun isn't even loaded," said Harry.

"Yes, it is!" insisted Bernie.

"Bet it isn't," said Harry.

"IT IS!"

"Don't believe you!"

"IT'S LOADED I TELL YOU."

"Prove it," said Harry.

Bernie aimed at the sky and pulled the trigger. An almighty boom from the gun sent birds to the skies squawking furiously: causing Harry, Jonny, Gloria, Huxley and the two guards to nearly jump out of their skins; causing Gossie, standing close to Bernie, to temporarily lose hearing in her right ear; causing King Chisel, Doctor Barbara Face-Problem and Honey Plunge back at the palace to look up from their cups of tea in alarm; and causing two startled goats to fall off the oak tree branch on which they were standing, Fortuna Piranha landing on Gossie Fountain and Rodney Dangertubes landing on Winston Bernard Alfonso Charles Gordon Gideon Demerol Smitherington-Piffle.

330

CHAPTER 55

King Chisel died three months later. Not, as Honey had always imagined, because of a fall or an accident of some sort, but peacefully in his sleep.

There was much sorrow throughout the land, for he had been a popular king despite his grumpiness, and the new king immediately called for three days of national holiday as a mark of respect. Honey herself was heartbroken and cried for a week. She'd loved

King Chisel even though he'd often driven her to distraction.

The coronation of the new king was organized to take place a fortnight later. Officials at the palace had been planning for it for years and were able to move quickly.

The big day drew thousands of well-wishers to the cathedral. It was a beautiful day and people thronged outside chanting their new king's name.

Inside, the place looked stunning. Huge bouquets of flowers, royal banners, a crowd buzzing with anticipation and a guard of honour looking dashing in their uniforms, beavers sitting proudly atop their heads.

There, in the front row, sat the new Minister for Science and Technology, Huxley Beeline, alongside his beaming mother and the new

Minister for Sport, Gloria Squat-Further. Next to them, the new prime minister, Honey Plunge, who had taken care to avoid chicken, sesame seed and spinach sandwiches, the royal physician Dr Barbara Face-Problem, and wearing a pair of velvet legwarmers and a leotard in the national colours, the recently knighted Sir Randolph LaTouche.

Two seats were empty. Bernie was still recovering in hospital, having broken his leg in a caprine accident. Once discharged, there was a cell waiting for him in the palace dungeon. Bernie insisted that he'd been at the beach on the day he was supposed to have fired the gun. Amazingly, despite multiple witnesses to the contrary, quite a few people believed him.

Gossie's seat was also vacant. She had

suffered only minor bruising in the goat incident but was too embarrassed by her recent behaviour to appear in public. She had, of course, been disqualified from the Crown Duels and she was genuinely sorry that she had allowed herself to be so badly influenced by Farting Bernie.

In the second row sat the families and friends of the Crown Duels contestants, including, of course, Jonny Mould's mother and father, beaming with pleasure, and six Mould cousins, each holding a piece of celery. Gloria's schoolfriends and teachers were all there, hands covered in chalk as a tribute to their friend.

Up behind the altar, Jonny and Harry peeked out through a gap in the curtain.

"I'm nervous," said Jonny. "What if they

don't like me?"

"They will," said Harry. "They'll love you. Are you ready? It's nearly time."

"Harry," said Jonny. "Thank you."

"For what?"

"For trying so hard to persuade me to be king. It was generous of you. Even though I caught Rodney Dangertubes after he crashed on to Bernie, and technically won the king's challenge – the minute I won, I knew being a king wasn't for me. I should never become king. How can I make radical art, how can I challenge the status quo, how can I speak truth to power, if I *am* the power? Thank you for understanding that. It wasn't right for me. Gloria felt the same – she loves sport, but she realized she was no leader. Huxley hated every minute of the contest and being king

335

would not use his talents properly. Only one of us really wanted to lead – and only one of us would be good at it. And that's you, Harry. You're smart and kind and you put others before yourself – that's why you'll be such a great king. You're the best choice; that became clear to *everyone*."

"Stop, you're embarrassing me!" Harry grinned.

"And, finally, thank you for allowing me to present my new performance piece at your coronation."

"Sure," said Harry. "It's the least I could do."

Harry couldn't resist one more peek out into the audience and at the third row, where G-Sponge, both his parents, Maddie, and Cy were sitting. All with enormous grins on their faces, bursting with pride, their money problems now a thing of the past.

"How long is your piece, by the way?"

"Oh, only about two hours," said Jonny as the lights dimmed and the audience quietened in anticipation. "The poem has about three hundred and twenty verses so, yes, should take me about two hours once you add in the dance, the chanting and the mime."

Harry tried to look pleased.

"I'm kidding!" said Jonny. "Your face! I'll be five minutes. This is your day. Go round to the front of the church and prepare for the procession. Wish me luck!"

Jonny slipped through the curtains and out into the light, and a smiling King Harry led the applause.

ACKNOWLEDGEMENTS

So look – I'm well aware this is the second of my books to place quite considerable emphasis and attention on farts and farting. And, given that this is only the third book I've written, that means 66.666% of my books concern themselves with that particular area of human activity. Them's the breaks. I'd like to state here and now that there will be zero farting in the next book. I'd like to but I can't. Let's see which way the wind blows.

Thanks to my super-talented and delightful sister, Anita, for once again so wonderfully bringing the characters to life. Seeing the illustrations for the first time is my favourite part of the process. As soon as I wrote about the beaver hats worn by the palace guards, I looked forward to seeing that particular drawing and it did not disappoint.

Thanks to Lauren Fortune, my editor, for her brilliant guidance, advice and encouragement; to Genevieve Herr for her invaluable suggestions and insight; to Penelope Daukes for getting the word out with such panache. Also Sarah Dutton, Bleddyn Sion, Aimee Stewart and everyone at Scholastic, thank you.

Thanks to Peter Nixon for getting me hooked on books, theatre and film when he was my form teacher all those decades ago and also for help with this book. And thanks to my agent Paul Stevens for looking after me so diligently.

Finally, thanks to my son, Harry, not just for lending his name to the lead character of this book but also for inspiring his decency and kindness. I'm a very proud father.

STEPHEN MANGAN is a Tony-nominated actor known for his roles in *Green Wing, I'm Alan Partridge* and *Episodes*. Stephen also voiced the title role in *Postman Pat: The Movie*. He was a member of the judging panel for the 2020 Costa Book of the Year prize.

@StephenMangan

Photo © Billie Charity

ANITA MANGAN is a successful illustrator and designer who has worked on award-winning books for the Leon brand, Gizzi Erskine, Fearne Cotton, Ella's Kitchen, Comptoir Libanais and the bestselling *'Be a Unicorn, Sloth, Flamingo...'* series.

@anita_mangan
@neeneelou

DON'T MISS:

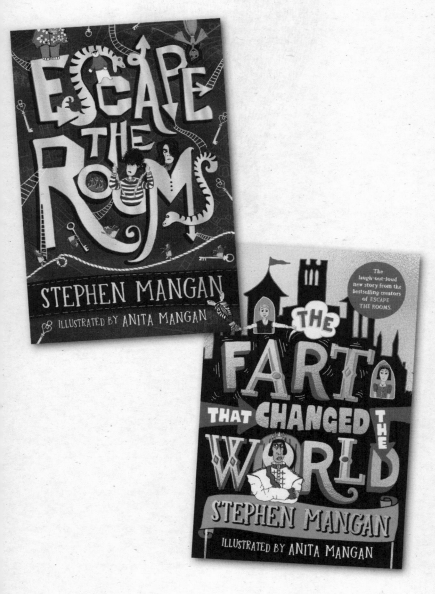

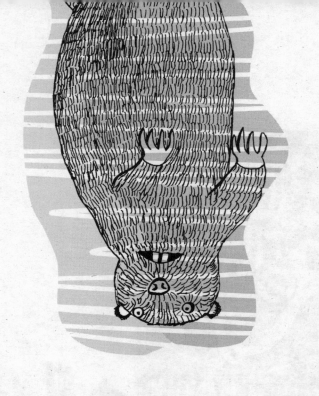